In *STAR LIGHT STAR BRIGHT*, Stanley Ellin introduces Johnny Milano—a New York private eye with Hollywood dreams caught in the Florida sun. In exactly forty-eight hours a man is marked to die. And for exactly twenty grand Johnny has been bought to save him. But between Johnny and the hour of death stand a few sensual and seedy characters, and the only woman who ever brought tears to the eyes of a man who's seen it all—Johnny Milano.

STANLEY ELLIN

STAR LIGHT STAR BRIGHT

BALLANTINE BOOKS ● NEW YORK

Library of Congress Catalog Card Number: 78-11519

ISBN 0-345-28541-7

This edition published by arrangement with Random House, Inc.

Manufactured in the United States of America

First Ballantine Books Edition: February 1980
Second Printing: April 1980

for Sue, with love

Star light, star bright,
First star I see tonight,
I wish I may, I wish I might,
Have the wish I wish tonight.

Not Blue Monday, as it turned out. Deep Purple Monday.

For openers, there was this necessary meeting with an exceptionally prosperous and ratty fence named Hennig, and at six-thirty that morning, a freezing January wind whistling through the dark emptiness of Lower Manhattan, we finally got together at the corner of Broad and Wall. We were no strangers to each other. I climbed into his shiny this-year's Continental and sat for a minute thawing out. When I could uncurl my fingers I handed him his fifteen thousand in hundred-dollar bills as specified, and he counted it with the dexterity of a racetrack cashier.

"The stones," I said.

"Not yet, Milano. I hear tell the insurance company coughed up thirty thousand for this item."

"So?"

"So I'm getting stiffed. Fifteen for your agency and fifteen for me is not how I see it." He neatly worked the packets of money into the depths of a brief case. "How I see it, there's another ten coming my way."

I said reproachfully, "Changing the rules in the middle of the game, Hennig? Do you know what that can do to your credibility?"

"You can knock off the funny talk, Milano." His hand slid out of the brief case with a gun in it, a snub-nosed, small-caliber piece. He held it low and aimed rather shakily in the general direction of my Jockey shorts. "No funny moves either."

A fence pulling this kind of strong-arm stuff? It was as much against nature as a cockroach suddenly rearing

1

up and showing a mouthful of teeth. I said, "Talk sense. You know I'm not carting any extra ten grand around with me."

"No?" He pretended great surprise. "So you take care of that soon's your bank opens. Then you phone me and I'll tell you where we close the deal." He sounded peevish about it. "Now, get going."

A roach with teeth, I tried to convince myself, is still a roach. I chopped my left hand hard down on his wrist, and the gun hit the floor under the brake pedal. We banged heads going for it, but I beat him to it. I dug it into the side of his neck. "We will now close the deal, Mr. Hennig," I advised him, and Mr. Hennig, moving very carefully, worked the plastic bag out from under his shirt. The necklace was a diamond-and-emerald job insured for 120 thousand and even through the bag it was a pretty thing to see.

I dropped the gun into a convenient sewer on the way back to my car parked around the corner. As it hit bottom with a splash I realized that, arctic wind or no arctic wind, I was soaked with sweat.

At seven o'clock, on schedule, I handed over the necklace to Elphinstone, the insurance company's man, in the suite he had rented for this purpose at the Plaza. A snowy-haired Ivy League type outside, another Hennig inside, he laid the jewels on a square of black velvet and, loupe in eye, checked off each piece. "All present and accounted for," he said at last. He gave me a smiling once-over, obviously working up to something significant. "I'm sure you realize, Milano, that you've built up an exceptional record on my company's behalf the past couple of years."

"Yes?"

"An exceptional record." He turned up the condescension another notch. "It leads me to wonder how you'd feel about leaving your agency's payroll and coming on ours. With a healthy increase over your present pay check, of course."

I said, "Nice of you, but I'm not on the agency's payroll. I happen to be a full partner in Watrous Associates. I'm the Associates."

2

"Oh?" He looked blank. "Mr. Watrous never mentioned that." He instantly reverted to type. "Well, well. In that case I imagine you're doing very nicely for yourself as it is."

"Very. But even if I weren't, I wouldn't sign on with you, Mr. Elphinstone. You see, the man I just dealt with knew exactly what you were paying to reclaim this trinket. Including my agency's fee as go-between. Which means that you are extremely careless about how loud you swap company secrets with your buddies at the local saloon."

He poked a finger into my chest. "Now, look here, Milano—!"

I brushed the finger aside. "Careful, Mr. Elphinstone, I'm very touchy right now about anything being pointed my way, even fingers. And next time you call on me for one of these allegedly confidential jobs I may or may not answer, depending on my mood of the moment."

At nine-thirty, allowing time for bath, breakfast, and a too-brief nap at the apartment, I was behind my desk at the agency. I had come in through the private entrance, but Shirley Glass, office manager and Mother Carey to Watrous Associates since its birth ten years before, had her antennae tuned in to the least vibration within these walls. She walked in a minute later, dropped the weekend's collection of investigators' reports on my desk, and drew open the curtains exposing the floor-to-ceiling windows and a sky which, at least from East 60th Street northward, promised snow. She said, "How about Hennig?"

"All settled. Any calls?"

"Only two that count. One was your sister Angie. It seems you were supposed to be out in Brooklyn yesterday visiting your mama and her, but you never showed."

"Because Hennig kept me tied to the hot-line all day until he made up his mind when we'd meet. We didn't get together until a couple of hours ago."

"I thought as much. So will you please tell Angie to quit playing hotshot lawyer with me? And always mak-

3

ing me stand witness for her worthless thirty-eight-year-old kid brother?"

"She is a hotshot lawyer," I pointed out. "Ask the Legal Aid Society. What was the other call?"

"Kind of interesting." Shirley gave me a slantwise look to make sure I was tuned in. "From Miami. From a Mrs. Andrew Quist."

"Sharon Bauer?" I said when I could bring myself to say it.

"Sharon Bauer Quist," said Shirley. "Don't forget the Quist."

"What'd she want?"

"What did she want last time around? Your professional services, so she said. It seems there's a murder in the making down there in Quist country. You're to come right down and stop it from happening. So she said."

"But you don't believe there is any murder in the making."

"Oh for God's sake, if there is, there's Miami agencies she could call in. And in case you forgot, she now happens to have a billionaire husband who could rent the whole FBI for her." Shirley snatched a cigarette from the pack on my desk. She scorched it halfway down its length lighting it. "That was at least three years ago, wasn't it, Johnny? I mean, you and her."

"About."

"Enough time to show you the way it really was, right? The hottest production of *Romeo and Juliet* ever put on, except in this one Juliet all of a sudden dumps Romeo. So for the next two months he's an emotional basket case."

"Don't push it," I said. "It was no two months."

"Two months by my calendar before you stopped crawling in here every morning half-stoned. When you did get yourself together I figured she was out of your system for good. When you sent back those letters of hers without reading them I was sure of it. You mean I was all wrong about that?"

"No."

4

"Then prove it. Tell me right out that when she calls again you want me to put her on hold permanently."

"Consider yourself told," I said. "Now, I've got work to do."

So there I was, plowing through a stack of reports, none of which made much sense to me because I was undergoing a Proustian effect in reverse. For my old buddie, Marcel Proust, a certain scent in the nostrils triggered vivid recollections of the past. Now I was vividly—too vividly—recollecting the past, and the recollections were sending up to my nostrils a certain perfume. The whole room was saturated with it.

Sharon Bauer Quist. Sharon Bauer. Her perfume— the only kind she used—was Fleurs de Rocaille, and her way of using it was simply to drench her underclothes with it. Nothing else, nowhere else—just a reckless dousing of it all over that minimum of brassiere and panties, take it and like it.

I was taking it in now with every breath. I hated it.

A few minutes after eleven the spell was broken when my partner strolled into the room, trim and beady-eyed as a winning gamecock. Crowding seventy, high-priced clients lining up at the door, a police lieutenant's fat pension for lagniappe, he had it made, had Willie Watrous, although he could never bring himself to really savor it. The compulsion to accumulate money made him mean-spirited.

A deliberate man, he settled himself in the chair across the desk, relit the stump of fifteen-cent cigar in his jaw, brushed ashes from the lapels of his synthetic tweed jacket. He said, "Shirl tells me it went all right with Hennig."

"It did. After I took a gun away from him."

Willie looked mildly surprised. "He pulled a gun on you? Why would he do a stupid thing like that?"

I told him why. Then I said, "Now that you're here, Willie, I'm unloading these reports on you. I can't focus on them with that gun on my mind. Better if I just take the afternoon off."

Instead of going into his Edgar Kennedy slow burn at

5

this he nodded sympathetically. "Having a gun aimed at you can do that, Johnny Boy. But why only this afternoon? How about a couple of days tanning up in some nice tropical sunshine? First class all the way, and everything on the house."

The usual sarcasm, of course. Then a light dawned. "By any chance, Willie, did you just get a call from Miami? From an old girl friend of mine?"

"Not exactly." He slid an envelope across the desk. "Take a look."

I took a look. In the envelope was a cashier's check for twenty thousand dollars issued by the Central Manhattan Trust Company. I looked closer to make sure. The check was still for twenty thousand dollars.

Willie said, "A bank messenger showed up half an hour ago with that hunk of paper. Also with a Miami number to call. So I called. It was Mr. Andrew Quist, the big man himself. It seems his wife's been trying to contact you, but no dice. So now he was depending on me to deliver the goods."

"And I'm the goods."

"You are. There's trouble down there, Quist said. Letters threatening a murder. So you—nobody but the champ himself—are invited to go down for a couple of days and clear things up. Just two days, and that's it."

"At ten thousand a day? And why just two days?"

"Because those letters pinpointed the time the killing is set for. This Wednesday midnight. Just make sure there is no killing, Johnny Boy, and Thursday noon you're back in your own little nest on Central Park South."

"And who's supposed to be the victim in this thrilling drama? Mr. Quist or Mrs. Quist?"

"Neither. He has this estate down there—Hesperides, it's called—with a houseful of company in it, and it's one of them got the black spot. Anyhow, he'll explain it all when you get there. That means today. There'll be a limousine waiting outside your apartment at two o'clock, then his private jet, then his car at the other end. First class all the way."

6

I said, "First-class travel is one thing. Twenty thousand cash for two days is another. It's way too much, Willie. It's panic money. I can't see a man like Quist going into any panic about the kind of foolish situation he described."

"So you say. But from what he said, his wife is sure as hell in a panic. And I got the idea that anything the lady wants, the lady gets."

"Is that his picture of her or yours?"

Willie snorted. "Ah, come on, Johnny Boy, why do you think she ditched you and wound up married to Daddy Warbucks? A sixty-year-old wheelchair case like that."

An honest, if painful, question. After three years, it deserved an honest answer.

"Why?" I said. "Because her astrologer told her to."

Willie's lip started to curl. Then, taking in my face, he uncurled it. "Her astrologer?"

"A hustler named Kondracki who started off by reading horoscopes for a lot of show biz people like her. Along the way he lined up his favorite pigeons in some kind of mystic cult where he was really in control. Get it straight, Willie. She didn't just wave goodby and walk out on me that day. She cried a bucketful and puked up her breakfast and then told me the Master had given her marching orders. So she marched."

"Jesus," said Willie, "you never let me in on that part of it."

"I'm doing it now so you can appreciate the kind of screwball she is. And why I've had this feeling she never really wrote me off." I waved the check in front of him. "Right this minute I have that feeling full voltage."

"Ah, now you're talking like a screwball yourself, Johnny."

"She has that effect on people."

"Not on me." Willie shook his head grimly. "You might be ready to kiss off this twenty grand, but half of it happens to be mine, partner. You want to give charity? Fine. Just give out of your own pocket."

7

"It's not a matter of charity, Willie."

"Oh yes it is." His face was reddening. "It's the same as those lousy I.D.C.'s you're so big on. We got a dozen investigators getting fat off our payroll, and two or three of them are always on that kind of useless job. You want me to keep playing along with any such bleeding-heart, red-ink operation? All right, you get ready for a quick trip to Miami, and I'll figure we're all even."

I had been waiting for him to sooner or later cut loose about those I.D.C.'s. They were the Indigent Defense Cases—the criminal investigation cases for the down-and-out suspect—which the courts would toss a hungry agency for a maximum three-hundred-dollar fee. Somehow, my sister Angie by woefully appealing to my tattered conscience had gotten me to take on a steady stream of her Legal Aid cases for Watrous Associates, a distinctly unhungry agency. And every I.D.C. client, considering the agency's quality work and high fees, meant a dead loss on the books.

My partner gnawed on the remnant of his cigar, watching me weigh the undeniable justice of his ultimatum. Then he said explosively, "What is this? Are you really scared to meet up with that dame again? Even with twenty thousand bucks riding on it?"

"Maybe."

"Maybe. Does that mean maybe you're scared you'll wind up in bed with her again? Or maybe you'll be tempted to beat the bejesus out of her?"

"Maybe both," I said. "Not necessarily in that order."

"Well, it won't be either one of them, partner. That check goes into the bank. And you'll go down to Miami. And when you're around Mrs. Andrew Quist you can keep your fists tight in your pockets and your fly zipped up. It's that simple."

"For you, Willie. Not for me."

"No? Then pay me off for my half of this check. And once and for all get off my back with those I.D.C.'s. Does that make it any simpler?"

It did.

Besides, how would I know if Mrs. Quist was still addicted to Fleurs de Rocaille if I didn't get close up to her one more time, even with fists tight in pockets and fly zipped up?

At Miami International the pilot of the *Quistco II* himself, the plane's steward trailing after us with my bags, led me outside the terminal building to a Mercedes limousine parked in the middle of a No Parking area and introduced me to Quist's emissary. This was a swarthy, grayhaired Hispanic gent, Virgilio Araujo, built low to the ground and wide like one of those pro ball carriers who can always be counted on for short yardage when needed.

Araujo saw me into the car as the chauffeur stowed away my luggage. When he got in beside me I said, "You're Security, right?"

"What gave you that idea?" The colloquial English was pleasantly Spanish-flavored.

"Shoulder holster," I said. "A nice fit, but it shows."

He smiled broadly. "Security, right. Chief of security for Mr. Quist in this area."

"This area?"

"The estate itself. Hesperides, that is. The duplex in town. The Quist Collection. Some commercial buildings. Some undeveloped properties to the south."

I remarked that this sounded like a large order, and he acknowledged that it was, what with well over a hundred personnel in his charge. What made it a little easier was that he signed on only high-quality stuff, no beach bums. He pronounced bums as bombs.

I said, "And I'm sure you have close connections with the local police?"

"Very close."

"Which leaves only one question. Considering the security you can provide, what am I doing down here?"

"You haven't been told that?"

"I've been told about some threatening letters. But to someone like your boss crank letters are a way of life. I'm sure there's procedures you've worked out for handling them."

"Naturally. But these aren't your usual crank letters."

"How about a practical joke?"

"I don't think so."

"Let me explain something," I said, and the look of amusement on Araujo's face stopped me right there.

"Let me explain something, Mr. Milano. The first letter appeared Monday, a week ago. When the second appeared on Thursday, and Mrs. Quist suggested calling on your services, I had you and your agency checked out."

"Obviously we passed the test."

"With high marks. But that means I know much about you, while you know nothing about me. For one thing, that I've had long experience in this kind of work."

"Private agency?"

"Before my employment by Mr. Quist, public service. In Cuba I was a security officer for the government."

"Interesting. Fidel's? Or Batista's?"

"Many years for Batista, a few months for Fidel. Both could tell you I was expert in my duties."

Araujo shrugged. "If you're curious about my political opinions, I'm glad to offer them. Batista was totally corrupt, of course. But hand him a share of your take, and your life was your own. Fidel? A fanatic who really believes that for their own good every Cuban must become his personal slave." He was warming up to his subject. "But when we replace him—"

"We?" I said jokingly. The joke went right past him. He said, "Believe me, there are plenty of us here in the States who still have the spirit to make a free Cuba again. And hundreds of thousands in Cuba only waiting for the chance to follow our banners."

"Not this week, I hope. I'm sort of counting on your fulltime cooperation for the next couple of days."

This seemed to haul him partway down from Cloud Nine. He said good-naturedly, "No problem there, I assure you. But in all seriousness, once the liberation is properly funded, who knows when the ax will fall? A question of money, right? And such questions have a way of providing their own answers, don't they?"

"Not in this business of threatening letters," I said, hauling him the rest of the way down to earth. "Two of them."

"Three. It was after the third arrived that the firm decision was made to call on you."

"Mrs. Quist's decision?"

"With Mr. Quist's agreement. Having checked you out, I thought it a sensible move."

"And how about our friendly local police? Invited to the party, too?"

Araujo shook his head. "Not unless we want this unpleasantness leaked to the press. Which makes it absolutely out of the question." He made a sweeping gesture with his hand, palm down, to indicate how absolutely.

"Mr. Quist's policy?"

"Yes, Troublesome for me sometimes, but necessary. I've seen what newspaper and television people make of any personal stories about him that come their way. Understand me, Mr. Milano. He's extremely well-balanced—tough but fair, isn't that how they put it?—but naturally he's highly sensitive to the way journalists choose to treat his private life."

"Naturally," I said. "I can remember those news stories about his marriage."

Araujo froze momentarily. He gave me a quick hard look, and I gave him a full view of my sympathetic face. He thawed. "His marriage. Yes. But as to why I believe these murder threats are no joke, there have been incidents supporting my judgment."

"Such as?"

"For one thing, the butchery of a dog. Mr. Quist's pet. Its throat was slit. That was on Thursday after the receipt of the second letter. On Friday, a carving knife from the kitchen, its blade encrusted with dried blood—I'm sure it was the knife used to kill the dog—was found driven into the door of the intended victim named in the letters. Does this pattern suggest a joke?"

I said that, well, I wouldn't want to bet on it either way, but it did smell of an inside job. Was it possible that among the staff serving the estate there was a psycho running loose? Had the staff been checked out one by one?

Araujo nodded emphatically. "Better than that. Friday afternoon, I gave every one of the staff—service people and Security—a week's paid leave of absence. With Mr. Quist's approval, of course. By Saturday noon, all were replaced by personnel I'd stake my life on. Then yesterday, despite these precautions, the third message appeared."

"Yesterday? Sunday? Then it wasn't sent through the post office?"

"Neither were the others. The daily mail is left at the gate-house and brought by the man there to the main house. The first two messages were among the letters left on the foyer table in the main house, but unstamped, obviously just dropped there. An inside job? No question. But at least it reduced my list of suspects to those guests resident on the estate yesterday morning."

"How many does that make?"

"Seven in residence. Since one—a Mr. Daskalos—is marked as victim, that would leave us six suspects. He also stands apart in another regard. He is the only guest not in the movie business."

"I see. So we have six guests under suspicion. And I'm supposed to gracefully mingle around and see if I can't finger the menace. Is that it?"

"Yes. And remember this. You can be quite direct in your investigation."

"No objections from the customers?"

"Movie people," Araujo said. His tone made it plain what he thought of movie people. "They're hoping Mr.

13

Quist will invest in a production they plan. Knowing he requires their cooperation with you, they will at least make a pretense of cooperating. To put it plainly, Mr. Milano, they will eat shit for the sake of their precious movie."

The Mercedes was traveling on an expressway eastward away from the airport. This section of Miami—low buildings bathed in pink sunset, palm trees—made a nice Chamber of Commerce picture.

Araujo said to me, "You've been here in Miami before?" and I said that, no, I had handled a case in Palm Beach long ago, but that was as near as I had gotten. Then I said, "Six suspects. Any of them deserve special consideration?"

He scratched his jaw thoughtfully. "Well, two of the guests are ladies. I'd say that the killing of the dog—a large and active animal—makes those two unlikely suspects."

"What about a partnership? One of the gentlemen kills the dog as, let's say, a favor to one of the ladies?"

Again Araujo gave me that quick hard look. "I didn't think of that. It may be worth thinking about."

The car looped south onto a fairly narrow road. The subtropics, lush but seemingly well-tended, pressed close on both sides here. Old Cutler Road, according to a street sign that flashed by. Across the road the subtropics became a long high fieldstone wall which seemed to go on endlessly.

Araujo gestured at it. "Hesperides. Some years ago an association of very rich gentlemen built it as a—what would you call it?—a private club, I suppose. When the venture failed it was put up for sale. Mrs. Quist liked it, so Mr. Quist bought it for her."

We pulled through wrought-iron gates and stopped beside a gatehouse. A guard gave Araujo a respectful hello, then took the key the chauffeur handed him and lifted the trunk lid for a quick inspection. From where I sat I had a view of rolling lawns, flowerbeds, avenues bordered by royal palms, and in the distance, a complex of fieldstone buildings which gave the impression of a blueblooded New England college transplanted all of a piece to this humid and garishly sunlit clime.

"Well," Araujo said, "what do you think of it?"

"Mr. Quist certainly bought Mrs. Quist a nice present," I said.

It could have been the lobby of an old-fashioned grand hotel minus registration desk. An abandoned hotel, not a soul in sight. Then a lithe young man appeared, dressed in what would seem to be the house uniform: white shirt, black bowtie, gray corduroy vest with scarlet piping and matching slacks. Vest and slacks were tight enough to make the most of what was unquestionably a very pretty young man. He smiled engagingly at Araujo, ducked his head at me. "Mr. Milano?"

"Who the devil do you think it is?" Araujo said. "And don't tell me you didn't hear the car outside."

"Sure," the young man said cheerfully. "But I was with Mrs. Quist getting told what to do about Mr. Milano. I'm supposed to fix him up in his rooms."

"Pablo," said Araujo dangerously, "you don't fix people up in their rooms, you show them to their apartments." He said to me apologetically, "With the regular staff gone for the week, you understand, the quality of the service—"

I told him I was sure it would do fine, and he said he hoped so, and that we'd get together later in the evening. I traveled up one flight with Pablo and my luggage by elevator. On the way, I said to him, "Ever hold down this kind of job before?"

He grinned at me. "Nope. But you got to start somewhere."

"That's what they tell me." The long, wide, deeply carpeted corridor one flight up showed no more life than I had met downstairs. "Where is everybody?"

"The help?" Pablo said. "Here and there. Kitchen, dining room—"

"The guests?"

"Oh, them. Probably getting ready for prayer meeting down on the beach."

"Prayer meeting?"

"Sunrise and sunset every day near the boathouse. Mr. Daskalos runs it."

"He's a minister?"

Pablo said cagily, "You better ask him." Alternate doors along the corridor were numbered. Pablo pulled up before number 28, pushed it open with his foot. "This is it."

It was a sitting room, and as soon as I walked into it I had a powerful sense of déjà vu. Then I caught on. The room, spacious and high-ceilinged, could have been the one at the Plaza where just twelve hours before I had dealt with Elphinstone, the insurance company's pet fixer. Luxuriously furnished in what might be called streamlined baroque, here were the same crystal chandelier, the same sweeping drapes at the windows, the same tiled fireplace. One difference. This was obviously a working fireplace with kindling and logs stacked beside it.

The bedroom continued the motif but provided among the pieces a glossy TV console, and on the bedside table, a telephone. Pablo opened doors to offer a view of bathroom, dressing room, and walk-in closet, all on Brobdingnagian scale. "That's it," he said. "You want anything, just phone." He picked up a typed sheet of paper from the bedside table. "It's all down here. Room service, garage, whatever." He pointed at a folder on the desk. "Everything else is in there. Like the guest list and their rooms and phone numbers."

"And Mr. and Mrs. Quist's number?"

"Private. But you call their secretary, she'll connect you. That's Miss Riley." He reached for the phone. "Want me to put a call through?"

"Don't bother. Do you know where Mrs. Quist is right now?"

17

"Getting ready for prayer meeting, I guess."

"Well, whatever you guess, you find her and tell her that Mr. Milano has been on the move for the last forty-eight hours. And if she wants to get a look at him while he's still awake, she'd better do it right now. Read me?"

"Yes, *sir*."

"Then take off," I said, and he took off.

I looked through the bulky folder on the desk. An automobile map of the Miami area. A handsomely detailed map of the estate. A room plan of the building I was now in, appropriately titled Main Building. A Xeroxed guest list. The list already had its eighth name added to it: Mr. John A. Milano, Main Building, 28. Most likely the work of the very efficient Miss Riley.

According to Araujo, six of the guests were movie people, but with one exception they weren't movie people whose names I recognized. The exception was Michael Calderon, Main Building, 24, which placed him right down the corridor outside. Calderon, that aging stud with the mandarin mustache and an acting range limited to sullen or more sullen, was, in fact, about as recognizable as you could be, right up there on the superstar level. And he had been leading man in the last Sharon Bauer film.

I examined the list more closely. Only one other guest was quartered in this building, a Mr. Sidney Kightlinger, Room 20. But Mr. and Mrs. Scott Rountree were stationed someplace called Cottage D. Mr. Lou Hoffman and Miss Holly Lee Otis shared Cottage C. Mr. Kalos Daskalos occupied Cottage A.

I spread out the map of the estate. Cottages C and D were on the waterfront to the southeast of the main building, Cottages A and B to the northeast. Midway between these two pairs were a boathouse and docking area. An additional point of interest: since Cottage B seemed to be untenanted, Mr. Daskalos of neighboring A had a lot of privacy for himself up there in the northern reaches. And as designated victim, he'd be offering his assassin, if any, a lot of privacy too.

In the process of folding the map I caught sight of an

inscription in one corner: *Designed and Lettered by M. Riley Herself.* Efficient, talented, and with a sense of humor? Even without having cast an eye on her I was on my way to becoming a fan.

Keeper of the keys too. Want to black Sharon Bauer's eye nowadays, you had to phone M. Riley for an appointment.

The first time I had ever met Sharon Bauer in her pot-reeking rented London flat off the King's Road, she had a gaudy black eye under those oversized shades. And a shiny weal on her cheek and a split lip. That was the handiwork of her agent, a racketeer *manqué* named Frankie Kurtz who, with the completion of her previous picture, discovered he was slated to be her ex-agent and didn't like it. His game plan in response was simplicity itself: first blackmail, then a forged contract, finally the muscle. Flabby as he looked, he did have muscle.

To give him his due, he had taken an eighteen-year-old kid who was sweating out walk-ons in TV commercials and gotten her up the initial rung of the golden ladder. This he achieved by lending her out for one-night stands to anyone with movie clout until he lined up her first picture deal. That first picture made waves. The second—good story, good direction, and magical Sharon Bauer—made a tidal wave.

It was right after the third picture was completed in London that I got a call direct from the head man of Corinthian Productions—the agency had served him well in such matters over the years—to get the hell to London fast and untangle Bauer from whatever the hell she was tangled in, without a word getting out about it.

What she was tangled in, of course, was Frankie Kurtz, and it didn't take too long to comb him out of her hair and Corinthian's. She should never have fallen for the blackmail in the first place; the people she had been involved with were big enough and mean enough to have laid Frankie away for keeps if their names were dragged into the open, and Frankie knew it. The forged contract committing her to a life sentence as his property was so clumsily forged that he would have been hanged for it by any court that got a look at it. As for the muscle, I came to the conclusion later that week—thus adding therapist to my newfound roles of lover and surrogate father—that my girl must be made to understand that Frankie wasn't the only one ready and willing to use it. It took a little doing to get him up to that Chelsea flat, and with Sharon cowering against its locked door, to provide her with the necessary bloody demonstration.

But immediately after events in London were closed out, there were those two incredible weeks in the hideout in Devon. Johnny-and-Sharon time. Fourteen days. One fortnight. No pills. She had brought a big enough assortment of them in her jewel case to stock a chain of drugstores, and I simply dumped the load into the fire the first night. Light wines and beers were in order, but no hard stuff. No need for it, as I proved to her. All defenses down, all chemical trips canceled, it was just the total coming together, in bed and out, of Johnny-and-Sharon. Big Daddy and The Dependency Kid. Two dreamlike weeks of it, the only unpleasant interludes being those long distance calls of hers to her witch doctor in Acapulco, Walter Kondracki, once astrologer to the stars, now their coven master. I didn't know he ranked me until that last call on that last day. I woke up to it too late, sprinting after the Jaguar as it headed away from the house to the highway, wildly shouting her name until, pulling up winded, I stood there being soaked through by a pouring rain, trying to get a handhold on reality. Whatever it was, it certainly wasn't Johnny-and-Sharon. Or that pillow talk about whether she could survive life in bad old New York City, or whether I open a West Coast branch of the agency. Reality, in fact, seemed to be somebody named Walter Kondracki.

Kondracki.

Daskalos.

Prayer meetings? Of course, that would be Pablo's way of looking at it. But sunrise and sunset prayer meetings out there on the open beach?

A good question. And it started others ricocheting around my skull. Through them I heard a knocking on the sitting-room door, and I said, "Come in," and walked into the sitting room as she came in and closed the door behind her.

The Dependency Kid. Gila Bend, Arizona, was her birthplace, but a section of Gila Bend tourists weren't encouraged to visit. A drunk German handyman father, a slattern Mexican maid-of-all-work mother, but somehow when those Teutonic and Latin genes had gotten together they had made a miracle.

The miracle and I stood there looking at each other across the room, and I had a feeling that all we needed was Dooley Wilson at the piano, working his way through the vocal of "As Time Goes By."

I fixed my mind on the picture of her Jaguar heading down the lane to the highway, spraying wet gravel into my face. I said, "You're looking well, Sharon."

"You are too, Johnny."

"And now that we've cleared that up," I said, "answer one question. Is Kalos Daskalos somebody who used to be Walter Kondracki?"

"Yes." she said.

Ask an honest question, get an honest answer.

When she felt no real threat in a question she promptly became an honest-answer freak. That was why, when I suggested to Corinthian's P.R. man in London that I ought to keep her out of sight until those bruises healed up, he gave me his instant blessing. Otherwise, the international *paparazzi* would not only have photos of the bruises but also her candid explanation of where they came from. That P.R. man had gotten himself an ulcer trying to steer her safely through interviews and never quite making it.

The couch before the fireplace was long and wide. I stretched out on it, folded my arms on my chest, closed my eyes, and gave myself up to being tired. The tiredness was so bone-deep that it hurt.

"Johnny"—she was standing over me—"if you knew it was him, would you have come here?"

"For twenty thousand Yankee dollars? Why not?"

"Twenty thousand?" She sounded shocked. "Is that what Andrew said he'd pay you?"

"Already paid me. That's about seven dollars a minute. I worked it out on Andrew's personal jet coming down here. And the meter keeps running to midnight Wednesday."

"Don't talk like that, Johnny." One of the things about her was that voice, down there in the lower registers and always slightly hoarse. "And will you please look at me?"

I opened one eye barely enough to make out a blurred oval of face framed by dark hair. Glimmering sapphire-blue eyes. No nose to be seen through the blur. Laurencin used to paint them like that, no noses. A lightweight, Laurencin, but her women had a storybook enchantment.

I said, "What's with these sunrise and sunset devotions on the beach? Kondracki been born again? Or is he still playing guru to the softheaded set?"

"He's a guide to The Path. And those are Adorations." She said it very patiently, putting in emphasis where needed so that even a dull brain could absorb it. "And somebody here wants to kill him. Somebody is really out to kill him."

I said, "People who really intend to kill people just kill them. They don't work out a whole scenario which invites the victim to get out of range before the event. Most likely somebody wants to throw a scare into your Mr. Kondracki."

"It's not Kondracki. It's Kalos Daskalos now. It means 'the good teacher.' "

"Whatever. But if the good teacher thought he was set for execution here, he'd be gone already. Like me, however, he doesn't really believe it."

"But he *does*."

"All right, then why doesn't he just pack up and go? For that matter, why don't you all take off? That would close the case as soon as you're through those big iron gates out there."

"He won't go," Sharon said helplessly. "He's not afraid to die. He believes it's just part of The Path. And if he won't go, I won't."

"How about your husband? Doesn't he have any vote?"

"You don't have to sound so angry about it, Johnny. Andrew says this is his home, and he's not going to be driven out of it by any threats. You can't blame him, can you?"

I fumbled in my jacket pocket for my cigarettes, and she thrust her hand into the pocket and came up with the pack and my lighter. Along the way we made finger contact that shocked the tiredness right out of me. She

23

sat down on the edge of the couch, lit the cigarette and stuck it between my lips. There was no aura of Fleurs de Rocaille emanating from her. Just a body scent and warmth that was even more heady.

I said, "Why did you marry Quist? It wasn't money, I know that much. You were up to half a million and a percentage for your pictures, and you didn't know what to do with that. So what was it?"

"I had to marry him." She was being very reasonable about it.

"Of course. He chained you to the wall, heated up the irons—"

"Please. After you and I—"

"You split," I said. "Not I."

"All right, then. After that, I went to Acapulco and stayed with Kalos. We had our Gatherings there."

"Is that what they call it now?" I asked.

"It wasn't what you think. There wasn't any sex. Kalos doesn't approve of sex outside marriage. It was just believers in The Path getting together."

I said, "Where does Quist come in?"

"He has companies in Mexico, and they had a big party for him in Acapulco. Kalos took me there. There was a whole crowd around me, and then somebody came over and said Mr. Quist wanted to meet me. He was in a wheelchair and it was hard for him to get through the crowd. Then Kalos pointed at him and said to me: 'That is the man you will marry. Tell him so.' And I did. And that's how it happened. We were married that weekend."

I said, "I am dreaming all this."

"No. The Path led me to him, Johnny."

I said, "You must have been whacked out of your mind. You must have been flying right through the sound barrier."

She vigorously shook her head in denial. "No. Since we—Since that time in Devon, I haven't been on anything."

"No pills, no coke, no booze? Not even pot?"

"Nothing at all. Kalos is against anything that leads you off The Path."

24

I flipped the cigarette butt into the fireplace and draped my arm across my eyes to block out the sight of her. I said, "Your husband paid me twenty thousand dollars just to come down here for a couple of days to ease your fears. Can you imagine what he paid for that heartwarming introduction to you?"

"I thought of that afterward. And I asked him about it."

"Let me guess. He said there wasn't any payment."

"That's right." She pulled my arm away from my eyes. "Look at me, Johnny. Andrew said so. And Kalos said there must have been some evil force in me that made me even ask. Maybe there was."

I said, "There's an evil force in the Internal Revenue Service too. After you ran out on me I made a little study of the good teacher. Seems that the IRS had a lot of questions to ask him about undeclared income some years ago."

"I know about that. So does Andrew. But it all happened before Kalos found The Path."

I shoved her upright. Both my knees made popping sounds when I got to my feet. Seen in close-up this way, she had a clearly defined nose, short, straight, and flawless. And full lips, the lower perhaps a little too full. But then, hadn't some keen observer once remarked that in all great beauty there is some small imperfection?

I said, "Let's put aside the transcendental crap and talk sense. Whatever's going on here, your boy is better off elsewhere. There's a flight to New York at ten, and I can be on it with him."

"I told you he won't leave here, Johnny. Ask Andrew. He already had it out with Kalos. Will you please talk to Andrew right now?"

"No. First a couple of hours' sleep. Then Andrew."

Sharon said in distress, "But he's expecting you now. Besides, I thought you'd have dinner with everybody and get a look at them. Dinner's always eight o'clock here."

"On your way out arrange with somebody to bring me a personal wake-up call at nine-thirty and have a sandwich and coffee along. I'll see Andrew at ten."

"He won't like that, Johnny."

"Possibly not," I said. "But that's what can happen to a client who pays cash in advance."

It was Pablo who arrived with my wake-up call and my collation, an assortment of bite-sized finger sandwiches, each with a different-colored but similarly tasteless filling. I washed down a few of these samples of rich-man's junk food with tepid coffee and briefly considered, and rejected, a needed shave and a change to less rumpled clothing. It went against the grain to prettify myself for this first meeting with His Majesty.

According to Pablo, Mr. and Mrs. Quist occupied the south wing, ground floor. On the ground floor, which still looked as awesomely desolate as Grand Central at 2 A.M. I traveled south until I came to a transverse corridor displaying a series of massive doors. I knocked on the first one, and it was opened by a rangy young woman with a snubnosed, heavily freckled, very much alive face. Unkempt blond hair partly draping the face gave her something of a sheepdog appearance.

"M. Riley?" I said. "Cartographer and humorist?" and she said, "My God, recognition at last. It's J. Milano, I trust?"

I said it was and that the J stood for Johnny among my friends, and she said that the M stood for Maggie.

"Maggie," I said. "Fine. I like it."

"You probably like corned beef and cabbage too," she said, which, as it happened, I did.

She led me through an anteroom into the sitting room beyond. Sharon was sunk into a huge armchair there, her legs tucked under her, an orange-colored binder of papers on her lap. The London flat had been stacked high with these brightly colored binders. Movie scripts offered by the hopeful. Araujo sat at a table in the center of the room, brooding over a chessboard. On the other side of the table, backed against it, stood a wheelchair. Its occupant's bald, deeply tanned head, a horseshoe of close-clipped gray hair bordering it, was all I could see of him. Playing without the aid of a board, Quist was calling his moves with quick authority. Araujo taking his brow-furrowed time with each move, looked more and more gloomy about his prospects.

"Virgilio's good," Maggie confided to me sotto voce, "but it's no contest. It'll be over right quick." So it was. Araujo grunted to indicate surrender and irritably started to place the pieces in their case. The wheelchair was battery-operated, as I saw when Quist spun it around to confront me. He had a good face, tough and smart, strong-featured and deeply lined. Not a bad copy of a Roman senator out of Caesar's time who had seen it all and had, along the way, developed a finely honed sense of the ridiculous.

Sharon had predicted a stormy greeting from him if I held to my own schedule. Instead, he seemed apologetic. "I must have given you a long hard day," he said abruptly. He bore down on the arms of the chair and strained to get himself to a standing position. I was about to move forward and lend a hand, but seeing that the others remained unmoving I simply watched and waited. There were a couple of metal canes in a golf bag arrangement slung on the back of the chair. Balancing himself precariously, Quist drew them out, and with their help made his way the few steps toward me. He was wearing Bermuda shorts, and I couldn't help glancing down at those spindly, twisted legs supporting the heavily muscled torso. Quist caught the glance. "Rheumatoid arthritis," he said.

"Sorry."

"No more than I." We shook hands, and he had a powerful grip. "We can cut short the ceremony. Mrs. Quist, of course, is a most appreciative former client. Virgilio you've met. This is my almost indispensable Miss Riley. Now let's move the troops into action."

He steered me—there was some question of who was steering whom—to a seat at the table, then made his slow way back to the wheelchair. Maggie took a place at the table. I followed suit. Sharon hunched deeper into the armchair.

"Well," Quist said to me, "any ready-made solution to our nasty little problem?"

I said, yes, just get Daskalos off the scene.

"Except that he doesn't want to be gotten off," Sharon said from her chair, and Quist said placatingly over his shoulder, "Of course, dear. That's understood."

"Not by me," I told him. "And I'm sure I'm not the only one here who knows who and what the man really is."

"Who and what he was," Quist corrected, and Maggie remarked to the ceiling, " 'There are more things in heaven and earth—' "

I looked from one to the other. "Two votes for Mr. Daskalos? He does exercise that old black magic, doesn't he? But suppose I suggest, before I fall under the spell, that he's the one behind your nasty little problem."

Maggie looked blank. Araujo looked inquiringly at Quist. Quist looked inquiringly at me. "For what conceivable reason?"

I turned to Araujo. "Have you come up with anything that puts Daskalos outside suspicion?"

"No. But please understand. The kind of person he appears to be now—"

"Obviously a saint," I said.

Sharon came up behind Quist. She said to me, "Johnny, why make any such judgment before you've met him and the others? Or seen the letters. Or what happened to Rufus."

"Rufus?" I said, and Quist said, "The dog." He reached out and drew Sharon around to his side. "Dear, if we don't weigh every possibility—"

"Oh, please," Sharon said. "You know Kalos wouldn't hurt any animal, much less kill it. Or write freaked-out letters to himself. Maggie, where are those letters?"

Maggie plowed through the contents of an attaché case on a sideboard and returned with an envelope which she handed me. On it was typed *To K. Daskalos.* In it were three sheets of paper. I said to her, "Only one envelope?"

"This was the last one. Kalos didn't think of saving the others."

The notes were typed on heavy bond paper, a date at the head of each message, no signature following it.

Monday, January 16

I am in Hell. You have put me there and you must join me there. That will be the end of your Path. There is no return from Hell.

That opening sentence tantalized me. Faust? It certainly had a Faustian ring to it.

Thursday, January 19

What was done to the dog shall be done to you. Hell waits. Soon you will enter it.

I said to Quist, "Where was your dog killed?" and he answered with an effort, "In my office." He cleared his throat. "A brutal piece of work. But the note coming up is really the clincher."

Sunday, January 22

Now count the hours. Your final hour on earth ends midnight of this Wednesday.

I said, "Short and sweet," and Quist said, "At any rate, short. Did Virgilio tell you that on Friday a watchman here found a bloodied carving knife thrust into Daskalos' door?"

"He did. Also that you want to keep the police out of this. But if there are fingerprints on that knife—"

"None," Quist said. "Otherwise the police would have already been here to help identify them. If that's your point."

"Something like that," I admitted. "What about the typewriter? It doesn't take an expert to see that everything here's been done on the same machine—same dropped *o*'s and crooked *t*'s in each one—and if there's any possible lead to that machine—"

"Much more than a lead," Araujo cut in. All eyes swiveled toward Maggie. She said to me ruefully, "It's my machine. That dropped *o* and crooked *t*. My big old Hermes. I'm sure the stationery is mine too. Right out of my desk drawer."

I asked, "Where do you keep that machine?" but before she could answer, Quist abruptly said in the voice of exhaustion, "Show it to him, Maggie. And help any way you can." He turned to me, huge beads of sweat suddenly gleaming on his forehead. "I'll see you tomorrow morning in the Annex. At ten. Now, if you'll all excuse me—"

Company dismissed.

Steering me along the outside corridor Maggie said, "You have to understand that when he gets like that it means the pain's setting in. Bad."

"What's he do about it? Go heavy on the painkiller?"

"No, he won't let himself. Some mild sedative at most. And there's a Jacuzzi in his bathroom. And of course Sharon holds his hand."

"Would you rather be the one holding it?"

She broke stride for an instant. "Are you detecting now? Or is that a dirty mind spinning its wheels?"

"Not dirty. Devious. You might as well get used to it. Were you on Quist's payroll before his marriage?"

"A couple of years before. But let's get one thing straight. I've never had designs on Andrew, I've never gone to bed with him, I never expect to."

"That makes three things. Do all these doors along here open on Quist's apartment?"

"Most. Those are Sharon's rooms. The next are Andrew's. Then mine. But ease up, Milano." She stopped and faced me. "You just kicked over a large can of worms. I'd like them all back in place before we proceed further."

"Sure. I'm sorry I kicked over your worms, ma'am."

"You should be. It's not just that I respect Andrew too much to involve him in something smelly, it also happens that Sharon and I are totally *simpática,* and for very good reason."

"Very close friends?"

"Very. I'll admit it took time. When Andrew brought her home my first thought was, oh Jesus, here comes Hollywood. And what did she turn out to be? A little lost lamb. That's what you found out too, wasn't it, Milano?" She looked knowing. "And I'm not talking about her as just your client. I gather that was the least part of it."

"Do you mean she told you about us?"

"Who else could she tell? And when a female as vulnerable as that makes it with Sir Galahad she sure as hell yearns to tell somebody. But the point is that you know her at least as well as I do. So you must know I'm telling the truth about our relationship. Hers and mine."

I said, "It's people like you that make detecting easy. Where's Quist's office?"

"There." She pushed open a door, and when I remarked on all these unlocked doors providing ready access to evil-doers she said too sweetly, "But, you see, this isn't really the Hesperides Hilton. It happens to be a private home."

"A mighty big one," I said. "And that's a mighty big chip on your shoulder, isn't it?"

It served to cool her off. "Well, maybe so. But there's always been that talk about Andrew and me. And it always makes me so goddam mad."

"Don't let it," I said. "You ought to know that kind of talk comes with the territory."

Except for its handsome Oriental carpet, there was nothing luxurious about Quist's office. Plain business-like furniture, some file cabinets. Across the room, a pair of slatted glass doors showed a dimly lit area beyond. "A terrace," Maggie explained. "It runs the length of the building on this side."

"And I suppose that bleached-out patch in the carpet there—"

Maggie seemed mesmerized by it. "Blood. A whole pool of it. Her luck, Sharon had to be the first one to walk in on the mess. It really hit her hard. And Andrew was crazy about that dog."

"What kind was it?"

"Irish setter. A big good-natured slob if ever there was one."

"So Sharon was the first to walk in on the mess. Who was next?"

Maggie thought it over. "A couple of the help. Then one of them phoned the Annex, where I was with Andrew, to tell us, so I guess we were next. Then everybody else piled in here."

"What is this Annex?"

"Next building that way." She waved southward. "Gym, pool, sauna, the works. Closed to the public until noon. Andrew sometimes uses it in the morning, and he likes his privacy there. That's where you meet with him tomorrow."

"So he said. Would you know if anybody on the premises has a hypodermic outfit tucked away? Outside the staff, that is."

Maggie frowned at me. "Why?"

"Curiosity. Is there anybody here who fills that bill?"

"As a matter of fact, yes. Andrew for one."

"I thought you said he didn't use heavy drugs."

"He doesn't. It's for vitamin shots. The B-12 treatment. Not that it seems to help any."

"You said Andrew for one. Who else is there?"

"No big secret. The who else is a somewhat hardboiled lady named Belle Rountree."

I said, "Belle Rountree, Scott Rountree, Cottage D," and Maggie remarked approvingly that I had obviously been at my homework. She explained, "Scottie's a novelist and maybe screenwriter. It's his script that'll be made into a movie if Andrew signs the check. Belle is Scottie's wife. She's a diabetic. On insulin. She's loaded with those disposable hypodermics."

She waited for my reaction and looked baffled when I said, "I don't see any typewriter. Where do you keep it?"

"Right next-door in my own office. But don't you want to hear about the Rountrees? Or the others?"

"I just now heard about the Rountrees. What about the others?"

"Well, Sid Kightlinger's the producer who put this movie package together and wants Andrew to come in for half the costs. Corinthian Productions has already agreed to cover the other half if Andrew signs on."

"How much is half?"

"A million. And the package is Scottie's script he made from his book *Two Plus One*, with Lou Hoffman to direct and Mike Calderon to play the male lead."

I said, "That leaves a Holly Lee Otis, who's shacked up in Cottage C with Hoffman. For what I suppose are the obvious reasons."

Maggie nodded wisely. "And some extra. There are three big parts in the picture, and Holly Lee's in line for one. Not much more than a kid really, but rated a comer. At least by Lou Hoffman. To complete the package—or did Sharon already tell you about it?"

"About what?" I said, and Maggie said with raised eyebrows, "That she's supposed to play the main lead against Calderon."

"A comeback? And Quist'll go along with it?"

"If that's what she wants. And if the picture's made around here, not on the West Coast. That's no problem. Sid Kightlinger would shoot it in Greenland if she signs up. His favorite word for her is bankable."

"It's a word that has its charms. Now let's take a look at that typewriter."

Her office had the same layout as Quist's, same unpretentious furnishings, but it looked as if a lot of hard work went on here. Stacks of folders on every surface, well-filled bookcases, their contents in a disarray that suggested they were well-used. And unlike the other rooms here that I had seen so far, this one had pictures on the walls. High-quality reproductions. At least a dozen Van Goghs. A few Gauguins. A big one of Seurat's "Grande Jatte."

"Nice," I commented about the room in general, and Maggie said, "I used to think so too. Now it's a place where somebody keeps sneaking in to write sick messages. I can't even bear to use that machine anymore. I'll have to get rid of it."

"Not yet." I slipped a piece of paper into the Hermes and typed out a couple of test lines. I held up the paper before Maggie. "Sort of strains the eyes to read anything that pale, doesn't it?"

"I know," she said defensively. "I hate changing ribbons. I make a mess of it every time."

"When was the last time? A week ago?"

"I suppose. Somewhere around that."

I said, "Then you can stop worrying about people sneaking in here to write sick messages every few days. Those notes all have exactly the same pitch-black lettering, the kind you get from a nice fresh ribbon. Assuming you've been giving this machine a workout during the past week—"

"I have."

"In that case," I said, "we can also assume that those notes were all written at the same time. Probably last Monday."

Maggie puzzled over this. "Will that help you find out who wrote them?"

"I can't tell yet. But it does offer a profile of someone who's laid out a precise, long-range plan of action and is seeing it through step by step. Which means someone who's not quite the screwball those notes make him out to be. Or her."

"Her?" said Maggie. "Belle Rountree? Holly Lee? I don't think either of them—"

"Neither does Araujo. But for the time being we grant no exemptions. What we do is consider an interesting question. Why is the plan so long-range? Why did the note-writer allow nine days to H-hour? Why not just two or three at most?"

"All right, why not?"

I said, "A sadistic reason might be that this prolongs the agony for the intended victim. The trouble with that, according to you people, is that the intended victim isn't suffering any agony."

Maggie stared at me. "Would you like him to?"

"What's that supposed to mean?"

"That you never will forgive Kalos for breaking up what you and Sharon had going. So if anything does happen to him—"

I said, "I can see Sharon didn't hold back on that Sir Galahad story."

"No, she didn't. And the idea that you might deliberately let her down now when she—"

I cut in: "Lady, you do have a low boiling point,

don't you? But look at it this way. If Daskalos does get his throat cut, it'll make a hot news story from coast to coast. And I'll be in the middle of the story looking foolish. That would sort of depress me."

"I wonder."

"Me, too. About this typewriter, for instance. It's a beat-up manual, not a high-speed electric. And that's not shorthand in this steno pad here; it seems to be some kind of home-cooked Maggie system. So you're not a trained secretary?"

"No, I'm not."

"Then how'd you land this job with Quist?"

"Look, if you're working around again to the question of what Andrew and I—"

"It's late," I said tiredly. "And every minute it's getting later. Will you stop defending your honor—and Andrew's—and just answer the question?"

"All right, I was trained as an art historian. I wound up with a job in the Miami Library art department. I did some moonlighting for Andrew while I was there, research and such, and when he founded the Quist Collection he took me on as curator. The rest—the confidential secretary bit—came naturally. Satisfied?"

"If you are. Araujo also mentioned the Quist Collection. Is it on the grounds here?"

"No. It's in the original family home on Brickell Avenue near town. A mansion, really. Andrew spent a fortune having it converted into a proper museum. If it happens to come up when you're talking with him, watch yourself. It's a touchy subject."

"Why?" I asked. "Was he stuck with some fakes?"

"Not at all. But the public isn't allowed in. And now there's a class suit pending against Andrew demanding open visiting hours because of the tax exemption. He's sick about it. Especially since there was a case—"

"The Barnes case," I said. "Dr. Barnes, the Argyrol king. Had a great collection locked up on his estate in Pennsylvania until the courts made the heirs open it to the public."

Maggie gaped at me. "You know about that?"

"I've been there. It's a great collection all right."

She pressed her hand to her forehead. "Oh, God, I must have come on so poisonously condescending—"

"I'll survive it. I deal in art too, now and then. People have a way of stealing pretty pictures and, so to speak, holding them for ransom. Some insurers would rather have my agency handle the problem than the cops. Which leads me to wonder just how secure the stuff in the Quist Collection is. What's its estimated value?"

"About fifteen million. But Virgilio feels it is secure. He's the one who set up the system there: electronic and manpower." She did a double take. "You mean those threats against Kalos could be a way of having us focus on him while somebody robs the collection?"

"Stranger things have been heard of." I laughed. "The way you look right now, I think if you had to choose between somebody's throat being cut and one of those pictures being swiped—"

She said reproachfully, "Not really. But, well, there are a couple of those pictures—those Van Goghs—and all I know is that nothing must ever happen to them. Nothing."

"Sold on Vincent?"

"Completely. Desperately." She wasn't fooling about it.

"Is that why you're writing a book about him?" I patted the cardboard box beside the Hermes, half filled with typed pages, and I could see her tighten up. She said, "How do you know that's mine? How do you know it's even about him?"

"I assume it's yours because here it is. I assume it's about him because the name Vincent shows up all over this top page."

"Very observant of you. But it has nothing to do with why you're here. No, wait." She gave me a speculative look. "With your experience you could help out with some advice on it."

"Among art experts, lady, I am no art expert."

"Not that way. I mean as a professional investigator. An expert in searching out people and documents."

"Some other time."

"Tomorrow?"

"Tomorrow. In return for the offer, how about lending me some bedtime reading?" I looked over the bookshelves. "Anything here you'd recommend? Besides a life of Van Gogh?" The shelves at eye level were filled with books on art, most of them studies of Impressionists and Post-Impressionists.

Maggie motioned toward the lower shelves. "One of those possibly. But what about the knife? Virgilio put it away in the wall safe here. Don't you want to see it?"

"Well, my feeling is that when you've seen one bloodstained carving knife you've seen them all. I've seen one." The bottom shelves contained a hodgepodge collection of books on travel and exploration, and interestingly, a line-up of true-crime cases, several about the Jack the Ripper case. When I pointed at those and asked, "Another one of your favorite people?" Maggie said, "He's got to do with what I'm writing. I'll explain it tomorrow." And when I settled on a newish-looking book titled *Bligh and the Bounty* she pulled it out of my hand and replaced it with a Jack the Ripper. "Freshen up on it," she instructed. "It's relevant."

I easily put down any temptation to ask her how it was relevant. I said, "Will there be one of Daskalos' sunrise shows on the beach in the morning?"

"Uh-huh. If the weather is clear."

"Ah, yes," I said, doing a W. C. Fields. "Due to inclement weather Saint Kalos may not perform any miracles today," and I learned that when Maggie Riley smiled broadly she looked a fast sixteen years old. I said, "Anyhow, I want to be there. Have someone get me up in time for it."

"Sure." Then she asked soberly, "Mind if I confide something to you, Milano? Something highly personal?"

"I'm braced."

"All right, when Sharon insisted you be called in on this business, I thought it was the dumbest move possible. I mean, knowing so much about you two, knowing how she still feels about it—"

"Whoa, lady," I said. "Still is a very heavy word in that context."

39

"It's the honest word. Anyhow, knowing all that, I had a feeling she could be letting herself in for some dangerous complications if you did show up."

"I see. And now you've changed your mind about that."

"No," said Maggie, "I haven't. It's just that now that I've finally met you I can understand why she wanted you here."

I waited.

"That's all," said Maggie.

I was roused from sleep by the click of the lamp on my bedside table. I opened my eyes and found myself surveying by lamplight a great pair of legs. The legs were topped by hacked-off jeans. Above them was a bulky black turtleneck sweater. Above that was a freckled face leaning over me, half hidden by a curtain of long blond hair. "It's after six, Milano," said Maggie. "If you want to attend services, rise and shine."

When, showered and clothed, I went into the sitting room she was waiting for me at a wheeled service table. There was orange juice and coffee on the table and some slightly charred, heavily buttered pieces of toast. "Emergency rations," said Maggie as I sat down to them.

From the seeds in it, the orange juice was real orange juice. I said, "Last night you let it out that you and Sharon were—in your own words—totally *simpática*, and for good reason. What's the reason? Quist give you both a hard time?"

"Which is what you'd like to believe, isn't it?" Maggie said wickedly. "Especially about Sharon."

"Clever girl. What's the reason?"

She loudly crunched a piece of toast. "You know what Sharon came out of, don't you? Shantyville, Arizona? Brutal father, mother who screwed around?"

"Yes."

"Well, trade sand for swamp and that's what I came out of. Maggie Riley, girl of the Everglades. That's me. Except my father wasn't a childbeater, just a useless drunk. And my mother didn't screw around. She didn't

41

have time to. She was mostly in the county hospital getting parts removed."

"You've come a long way, baby. How'd you manage it?"

"The same as Sharon. But not with men. There was this art teacher in high school—a big old butch—who took a shine to me. Hooked me on art, hooked me on high living, like having a toilet right there inside the house, took me out of town on museum trips, dressed me up like her own pretty dolly. Helped me get the scholarship to Miami U. when the time came."

"In return for—?"

"That's obvious, isn't it? I didn't mind. In fact, it was highly pleasurable at times. Not that I ever bought it as a way of life." She looked at me quizzically. "How old do you think I am anyhow, Milano?"

"What's the difference?"

"Plenty. Because there's a poor-little-girl look in your eye, and I am no little girl. I'm thirty-three. Thirty-four next month. And very tough in my own way. When I was twelve I was already out with my daddy and my own rifle poaching alligators. And putting together a busted-down swamp buggy with baling wire and spit."

I said, "Tough and very touchy. About a lot of things."

"Like getting sympathy when it's not needed? Save that for Sharon. Emotionally, she's still back there in shantytown rubbing where it hurts. Unlike me, she never did get herself unscrambled."

"And you're big sister, trying to unscramble her."

"No," said Maggie, "I just listen and understand. And sometimes I say to myself 'There but for the grace of God—' " She looked at me steadily over her coffee cup. "I'll tell it to you right out, Milano. I think you would have been good for her over the long haul. I think it was a mistake for Kalos to get in your way."

I grunted something noncommittal and looked at my watch. I asked, "When does the curtain go up on his show?" and she answered, "Pretty soon. And you'd better wear more than that jacket. It's cold out. At least for Miami."

42

It was cold out for anywhere, a strong onshore wind making it that much colder. Although there was a graying of the sky to the east, the rest of it was dark, the stars very bright. We walked by the pale glow of ornamental gas lamps along a flagstone path across lawns, around shadowy flowerbeds, past a series of tennis courts, and it was a long walk. The end of the line was a wooden stairway leading down to the beach eight or ten feet below.

Maggie leaned back against the railing of the stairway. "Balcony seats," she said. The sea was running high, the waves breaking on the beach with a rhythmical boom and hiss. She had to raise her voice to be heard above them.

The sky ahead was showing pink now. On the water's edge in line with the stairway was a bathhouse and an L-shaped dock, a few small boats moored to it. Fifty yards to the north, on the grassy rise over the beach, was a handsome ranch house. That would be the empty Cottage B. Beyond it I could make out its mate, Cottage A, domicile of the good teacher. Southward were the other two cottages: the nearer where director Lou Hoffman and starlet Holly Lee Otis kept company, the farther housing the Rountrees. Cottages in Quist's enchanted garden, they would have been hundred-thousand-dollar homes on Long Island's north shore.

The sky reddened. From the southward buildings two couples emerged and moved in our direction. The Rountrees were both plump and on the short side. Hoffman and girl friend were tall and skinny. All were bundled up against the weather, all looked miserable. They came up in turn, surveyed me openly, and went down the stairway to the beach, making a semicircle there, facing the waves at a safe distance.

Maggie nodded a greeting over my shoulder, and I looked around to see that Quist and Sharon had made an appearance. Quist was in the wheelchair, a lap robe over his legs. Sharon, standing beside him, was swathed in mink. To her, mink coats—sable coats too—were a way of keeping warm. In Devon she used to play at gardening—awkwardly snipping, weeding,

43

digging—in a sable coat. Like Maggie Riley, girl of the Everglades, she too had come a long way, baby. But when she had suddenly cut and run that unbelievable morning she forgot to take the sable coat. Just left it lying there on our bedroom floor. I had a feeling that Maggie would never make that kind of mistake.

Further up the path a big, leather-jacketed man hove into view and took his position there. The black hair cut low across the forehead, the mandarin mustache, the craggy features added up to an instantly recognizable mask. Michael Calderon, superstar. Even more bankable than Sharon, if it came to that.

Sharon patted her husband's arm, then, without any sign of recognition, walked past Maggie and me and down the stairway. At its foot she shed her sandals and joined the semi-circle on the beach.

I put my mouth close to Maggie's ear. "Do they all show up like this every morning and evening?"

She shook her head. "Andrew hardly ever. Sid Kightlinger not at all. And we're not supposed to be talking. That's Kalos coming."

I watched him make his way down the beach. Seemingly anesthetized to cold, he wore the briefest of swim briefs. Middling height. A trim body. A mop of snowy-white hair. According to the record he'd be well into his sixties now. From the neck up he looked it. From the neck down he could have passed for twenty years less.

He stopped on the tideline directly ahead and faced the east, water foaming over his ankles. A sliver of sun showed over the horizon, grew larger. Daskalos turned to confront us. He raised his arms high over his head. "Adore this rebirth! Adore the light it brings! Adore the life it brings!" A deep commanding voice, although gusts of wind gave it a quavering effect.

Head back, he lowered his arms, holding them wide, making himself into a living cross. The sun continued to rise, as it will, and he continued to hold that position. It was a brutal position to hold. Bone-cracking.

The waves boomed and hissed. A flock of gulls appeared, dipped over the water, settled on the shore. A

44

gust of wind whipped Maggie's hair across my face. She grabbed the hair to hold it in place and mouthed "Sorry" at me. Calderon moved into my line of vision. He stood on the top step of the stairway now, watching the scene below with unblinking fascination, his fists slowly knotting and unknotting at his sides.

As the sun cleared the horizon Daskalos came to life again. "I am sent to guide you on The Path. Enter it— hold to it—and find peace." He extended his arms in benediction. "Peace."

That was it.

When I looked around, Calderon was gone. The two couples in the semicircle made their way up the stairs homeward bound. Sharon slipped on her sandals and followed. She came over to Maggie and me. If the good teacher had brought her peace, it didn't show on her face. She said to me, "Will you talk to him, Johnny? I think that's what he's waiting for."

He was obviously waiting for something, standing on the water's edge looking our way. Maggie muttered to me, "Hang on to your hat, friend, you're going for a wild ride." She hooked an arm through Sharon's, and they headed for Quist in his chair. I went down to the bottom step and decided against sticking my shoes into that sand. Daskalos took notice of this and walked toward me. It was even windier at this level than up above. I turned up my collar against the gusts and thrust my hands into my pockets for warmth. Also to indicate that I was not in a handshaking mood.

Daskalos didn't offer to shake hands. He said with a gracious dip of the head, "John Milano," and I said, "Walter Kondracki."

"I was," he acknowledged unperturbed. "And in that form a liar, thief, and swindler. And in that form long dead."

"Sorry I couldn't make it to the services. Anyhow, word is out that you're scheduled for another death very soon. You know I'm here to prevent that. If possible."

He casually dismissed the possibility. "Nothing can prevent it. We must die an infinite number of deaths.

45

But each death only means the release of the spirit into new flesh. And the new flesh, kindled by that spirit, may move all the more quickly along The Path."

"Beautiful," I said. "But no matter what sweet music you play on your sitar, teacher, angels are not being sent to snatch you away. Someone on the premises seems to have that job in mind."

"A servant of the angelic," Daskalos said.

"Or," I said, "could it be the ghost of Walter Kondracki playing games for some mysterious reason?"

"No, it could not." He looked at me, all compassion. "Are you really so afraid of death, John Milano, that you can't comprehend my not fearing it? Or my welcoming it?"

I said, "Look. I'm willing to address you by any alias you pick. I'm also willing, since I'm being paid for it, to try and keep you out of the county morgue. Beyond that, venerable one, get it into your head that I'm not in the market for your merchandise. If you can do that, it'll make life much easier for both of us."

"Will it? But why do you say you'll address me as Daskalos and yet seem to be addressing me as Kondracki?"

According to prescription I counted to ten before speaking. Then I said, "You son of a bitch, do you really expect me to forget who was on that long-distance line to England every day for two weeks? And what came of it?"

"Sharon made those calls, John Milano. She was entering The Path and saw that her arrangement with you might defile her. That it might be an obstacle in her way. Any such arrangement outside marriage is a defilement."

"I see. And her marriage to Quist was an act of purification. By the way, what was your rakeoff for playing Cupid, Daskalos?"

"A sense of rightness," he said unruffled. "Nothing more."

I said, "You just stick to that story as long as you can. Meanwhile, if you haven't been sending yourself threatening notes, I'd advise you to pack up your extra loincloth and get away from here fast. You understand I'm advising that in my professional capacity. In any other capacity I'd be delighted to just stand by and watch things happen."

"My death must happen. I welcome it. Believe that."

"We're talking about death by violence, Daskalos."

"Yes. And death by violence is always the end for the chosen one. A necessary sacrifice."

I said, "Let me get this straight. You are the chosen one?"

"I am. And when my mortal body is destroyed by an act of violence, as it must be, my immortal spirit enters another, and refreshed, again becomes the divine guide to The Path." He smiled at me beatifically. "Jesus Christ gave witness to this, John Milano. He was one of my manifestations."

The wind cut through my jacket and sweater. Sand stung my face. I consoled myself with the thought that this was still not as cold as the corner of Broad and Wall and that the smooth case I confronted was, unlike Hennig the avaricious fence, not packing a gun.

Enough was enough. I said, "It's always nice to meet one of the Holy Family, Daskalos. But getting down to cases, is there anyone around here who'd have some special reason for wanting to knock you off?"

"Please." There was a hint of impatience in it. "Even if I could name the one sent to end my present life, do you really believe I would do so? And defeat his necessary mission?"

He left me with that. And considering it must have been the same line he had handed Quist when first urged to be on his way, it left me with a fascinating picture of the confrontation between them. Especially that moment when Quist was informed that his now-unwelcome guest was, in fact, the most recent manifestation on earth of Our Lord.

Inside the entrance to the main building was a table bearing what appeared to be a shopworn silver punch bowl. Inside the bowl was a large assortment of mail which Araujo was thumbing through, piece by piece. He explained to me that further notes to Mr. Daskalos might be forthcoming, right? And much as he disliked getting this close to people's private affairs he felt it wise to check on the nature of each envelope as soon as the morning delivery was made. Too bad, but it couldn't be helped.

He took a long, roundabout way of explaining it, but I suffered no boredom, because at the elevator across the lobby a little scene was being played out by Sharon and Calderon. He, her fur coat slung over his arm, was talking intently. She, head down in reflection, was taking it in soberly. Then, in what might be interpreted as camaraderie by a clean-minded spectator, he casually slipped his free arm around her waist. She seemed unaware of it. That ground having been won, he lowered his hand and openly fondled her rump. She pulled sharply away, he contemptuously tossed her coat at her feet, stepped into the elevator and ascended out of sight.

Cut and print.

Araujo, who might otherwise have been entertained by this, was deep in the punch bowl. I gave him a polite goodby and strolled over to Sharon as she gathered up the coat. "You saw that, didn't you?" she said. She seemed more hurt than angry.

I said that, yes, I had seen it.

"Did Virgilio?" The possibility seemed to worry her.

I said, no, I didn't think he had. I pushed the elevator button and the dial over the door slowly pivoted from *II* to *I*. I said, "I hear you plan to make a picture with Calderon."

"It's not settled yet, Johnny."

"But if it does get settled, won't you mind having that stud all over you while it's being shot? You've already been through that."

She said defensively, "But nothing happened between us. And he's very supportive on the set. I need that."

He had been supportive. I had been supportive. Quist and Maggie Riley were supportive. Why not? Whenever one of her films had been released, a few million people—including ax-murderers, used-car salesmen, and politicians—sat in the dark, and as soon as she turned that face toward them, opened those lips and huskily spoke her first lines, they became instantly and passionately supportive. Who were we to be immune?

I said, "What were you doing here with Calderon anyhow? Don't you live over on the next block?"

"I was going up to your apartment and wait for you. I have to talk to you."

"We are talking."

"Not here," said Sharon. "Please." It was the kind of please that drove the ax-murderers, used car salesmen, and politicians right out of their minds.

My sitting room was thick with smoke. A quickly aborted fire had been started in the fireplace—wads of newspaper, a few sticks of kindling, a log laid over them—but the chimney damper was closed. I opened the damper, opened windows to let in salty gusts, while Sharon, handkerchief to nose, explained that she had told the boy to get fires going in the occupied apartments, but that he, like the rest of the present staff, was a temporary. She supposed he didn't know much about fireplaces.

"Pablo?" I said as we moved to the bedroom where the air was breathable. "Pretty as a picture?"

"I don't know their names. The new ones, I mean. But he was pretty, all right."

She sat on the edge of the freshly made-up bed, coat

49

draped over her shoulders, while I switched from sandy clothing to fresh. She said, "I have to talk to you about Kalos first. You've met him now. What do you think of him?"

"I told you long ago what I thought of him. Nothing's changed."

"Something has, Johnny. I guess I have."

She hit me with that while I was unbuttoning my shirt. The button came off in my fingers. "Changed how?"

"About The Path." She clenched her fists and pressed them together hard, the knuckles whitening. "I don't think I can believe in it anymore. Anyhow, not for me."

"You sure looked like a true believer out on the beach."

"I don't *feel* like one. If I hold to The Path I'm supposed to be happy. But I'm not."

"Do you and Andrew have a sex life going?"

"Yes, of course. It isn't that. The trouble isn't Andrew. And it isn't Kalos. It's me." She leaned forward toward me and said with slow emphasis: "I am trying to hold to The Path but I am not happy."

"Who is?" I asked rhetorically, but she had an answer all ready. "When we were together in England— after you got rid of Frankie Kurtz—I was. And you were."

"Sharon, that was three long years ago."

"I wrote you about it last summer, and that wasn't three long years ago. And you sent that letter back without even opening it. I wrote you Christmastime, and you sent that one back the same way. Why didn't you read those letters, Johnny?"

"I didn't have to, to know what was in them." I realized I was holding the shirt button. I tossed it on the dresser, pulled off the shirt. Sure enough, there was sand inside the collar. I busied myself putting on a fresh shirt.

Sharon watched me go through this. Then she said, "You couldn't have known everything in them. Not the important parts."

"Such as?"

"Well, that I wanted to go to New York and see you. And if it worked out, I wouldn't even come back here anymore."

"It wouldn't have worked out."

"Why not?"

"Because what's involved this time is not any pimping ten-percenter like Frankie Kurtz. It happens to be a highly respectable, obviously devoted husband. You've already played him dirty by getting me down here on his money. But at least I'm here on business. So we'll stick to business."

"Johnny—"

"No. Strictly business. Like, for instance, how you felt about that dog Rufus. Loved him dearly? Couldn't stand him? Indifferent?"

She looked puzzled. "What's he got to do with it?"

"Think it over. You were the one who discovered the bleeding remains. Now, what was it brought you to Quist's office at that time? When nobody was there."

It took her a few moments to catch on. Then she said incredulously, "Do you think I killed that dog? That I wrote those notes?"

"No. But there's certainly a case to be made for it."

"A case? What case?"

I said, "Consider the evidence. You were the only one at the scene of the crime about the time it happened. The typewriter and paper, and for that matter, the carving knife were readily available to you. As for motive, Daskalos has his hooks into you, and you just admitted that you're trying to pull loose."

"No, I didn't. Not that way. And what do you mean, he has his hooks into me?"

"You tell him everything, don't you? You always did. Every intimate detail of your life. Isn't that so?"

"Yes, but—"

"No buts. Sooner or later you had to realize you put him in the same happy spot Frankie Kurtz was in. That he could blackmail you silly."

She said hotly, "He's a priest just like the one in your

51

kind of church. Does your priest go around blackmailing people because they tell him everything?"

"That's an interesting comparison," I said. "All the same, if any hard-boiled cop added up what's going on here, he'd do a lot of heavy eyebrow-raising about you."

"That doesn't matter as long as you know I'm not mixed up in it. And you do know it."

"Yes. Which is why I suspect somebody may have set you up for these crude deductions."

She dragged the coat around her as if she suddenly felt a chill. "Who'd want to do that?"

I said, "How about Maggie Riley?" and when she seemed tongue-tied with disbelief I said, "Face it. She's had the same opportunities as you to pull off these Halloween tricks. And she'd have a solid motive for getting you into serious trouble with your husband."

"Maggie? What motive?"

"She was the lady of the house until you showed up. And for all she comes on so strong about never having screwed around with Quist, about having no interest in the prospects, that's highly arguable. Fact is, if she could make you a public embarrassment to him, she'd have plenty to gain, nothing at all to lose."

"Oh, man," Sharon said. "Johnny, haven't you been talking to her? Don't you know anything at all about her?"

"I thought I did. What don't I know?"

"For starters, that she was already married when I came here."

"I didn't see any wedding ring."

"All right," Sharon said impatiently, "she wasn't *married* married. But she was housekeeping with this guy. Donnie Maxwell. Taught art over at Miami University. Nicest guy you could meet. And they really made it together. Then last year, just about this time, he died. Just like that. Liver cancer."

"She never mentioned it."

"What did she talk about? Her book?"

"Only that she's writing one. I have a hunch the details will come as soon as she can pin me down."

"And she will," Sharon said. "She is really strung out on that book. That's how she started making it with Donnie. She got him high on that book too, and next thing they were both working on it together. But that's only part of it."

"What's the other part?"

"She's leaving here next month. She told me she put in for a foundation grant—the Lucas Foundation up in Boston—and it looks pretty sure she'll get it. To finish the book. She'll be in Europe two or three years at it. So screwing around with Andrew is sure as hell not on her mind. Or getting rid of me."

"I guess not."

Sharon got up and came over to me. She placed a hand on my chest and said pleadingly, "Kalos isn't behind this either, Johnny. Killing that dog was cruel. Those on The Path can't be cruel."

I said, "Your guru is a hustler. And hustlers have to be cruel or they're out of business. What I will admit is that I can't lay any motive on him for making trouble here. Nothing to gain in cash, credit, or coupons— which, no matter how you see it, is what he plays for. So we can sideline him as an entry, along with Maggie."

"And me," Sharon said drily.

"And you. But that setup theory might still apply. You were led for some reason to walk into that office right after the dog was killed, which is how these things are worked. First one on the scene. Now, if you were brought there by a phone call, whoever made that call—"

"But I wasn't. I mean, no phone call." She seemed flurried. "I went in to see Andrew. I didn't know he was gone already."

"You're sure of that? God'll get you if you're covering up for somebody."

"I'm not." She tried a smile. "No phone call. I'm sorry."

"It's too late to be sorry about it now," I said.

She dutifully went off to share breakfast with her husband in their apartment; I found my way to the dining room, which turned out to be just the right size and temperature for a hockey game. It offered a sideboard with the usual breakfast stuff laid on, and a long refectory table with highbacked, overstuffed armchairs like thrones drawn up to it. Lost in this vastness, two couples sat facing each other across the table. On one side, the short plump Scott and Belle Rountree, screenwriter and spouse; on the other, the tall skeletal Lou Hoffman and Holly Lee Otis, screen director and bunkmate.

Here the help outnumbered the guests. All were male, appeared to be Latin, and wore that tight gray corduroy with scarlet piping which suited lithe young Pablo so well, but which did very little for them. Two were at the buffet, two hovered over the dining table, two were in the remote distance holding a heated debate in an undertone. Dejà vu again. It could have been breakfast time in the restaurant of the Central Park South hotel I called home.

At the table while introductions were being swapped, I observed that aspiring screenwriter Scott Rountree was not so much plump as stocky, with a flattish face like an English bulldog; that redheaded, sharp-eyed Belle Rountree was flawlessly made up for the cocktail hour, which still couldn't conceal the fact that she had quite a few years' seniority on her husband; that cadaverous, middle-aged director Hoffman had a large bald area in the center of his frizzed hair and dark pouches under the eyes, the one perhaps having led to the other; and that Holly Lee Otis, an Alice in Wonderland type just out of her teens, was a girl who probably knew the score every minute of the game.

It was Holly Lee, mouth stuffed with Danish pastry, who patted the seat beside her and invited me to join the party. She also advised that in selecting breakfast I stick to corn flakes and Danish, because everything else was so rotten it was enough to make you puke. The coffee was all right, however.

At the buffet I followed her advice, and a hoverer brought back my order to the table and poured coffee for me. Holly Lee took this opportunity to order another Danish. A cherry Danish this time. "Jesus Christ," plump Belle Rountree said bitterly.

Lou Hoffman said to me, "Sharon Quist mentioned that you handled a very tough case for her in London a few years back. Nailed Frankie Kurtz for fraud. Peeled him off her back for keeps."

"Something like that," I said.

There followed a long meditative silence. I finished my corn flakes, went to work on the Danish. A cheese Danish. The outside was warm, the cheese inside cold. Frozen foods.

Holly Lee suddenly addressed me. "We saw you with Maggie Riley. What did she have to say about things around here?"

"Not much."

"It must have been more than that," Holly Lee said. "What do you make of that woman anyhow?"

"Feisty," I said.

"I meant—"

"And great legs," I said. "Marvelous legs. Nice posture, too."

"Oh, come on, Milano," Scott Rountree said witheringly. "You know why you're here. We know why you're here. How about getting down to cases?"

"Easy does it," warned his wife. She was eying the remains of the Danish on Holly Lee's plate. "Fuck it," she said. She reached out with knife and fork, cut herself a small piece and shoved it into her mouth. It was a replay of Bette Davis and the piece of chocolate in *All About Eve*.

"Belle!" said Rountree.

"Forget it, Scottie. I am cold, I am hungry, I am waiting for someone to commit a murder. My blood sugar is already up there in the high millions. It wouldn't even know the difference."

I frowned at her. "Do you really believe someone here intends to commit a murder?"

"Oh, yes. I've seen enough doggie blood flow to know that some kook among us is a real killer. And our prophet Kalos is asking for it. You put it all together, friend."

I said, "Do you mean Daskalos is asking to be killed so he can be resurrected? Or that he's steamed up somebody here to the point of killing him as a payoff?"

"And what a lovely payoff," said Belle.

Holly Lee was suddenly pinch-lipped and narrow-eyed. Lou Hoffman hastily laid his hand on hers. He said to Belle, "How about a little sensitivity on the subject? Remember you're not only among those who don't believe, but also among those who do. And those who are searching."

Belle said, "Your prose really sings, Lou. It sounds almost as Biblical as those notes the prophet's been getting."

Holly Lee shoved back her armchair, which wasn't easy, considering its dimensions. She stood up and looked down at Belle. She said very slowly, "You are a short, fat horse's ass," and stalked off with hauteur. Hoffman, looking distressed, immediately followed. The hoverers made a racket clearing away their table settings.

Rountree pulled out a pipe and some cleaners and with great concentration started a disassembling and cleaning job. His eyes on his work, he remarked to Belle, "Lou was right. You were wrong."

Belle gave me a wry smile and dipped her head in her husband's direction. "A searcher," she informed me.

"An observer," said Rountree.

"Oh?" said Belle. Then she said to him in a singsong, "Forgetting that he who observes too closely may get nose bitten off." She nodded solemnly at me. "Present company excepted, of course."

I laughed. "Well, I have to admit that my line of work . . . Anyhow, I gather that Miss Otis and Mr. Hoffman are Believers."

"Not Lou," said Rountree. "Not anymore."

"But the way he talked—"

"Only because of Holly Lee." Rountree assembled the pipe and blew through it.

Belle explained: "Lou used to be one of the faithful. That's until Kalos steered Holly Lee to him, and he gave her a part in his last picture. It wound up with Lou moving out on the wife and kiddies and in with Holly." Belle shrugged. "Yet another aging male suckered by the find-your-lost-youth syndrome."

I asked, "Why would any of that stop him from being a Believer?" and Rountree answered, "There's a moral code involved. A very rigid code. Did Maggie Riley tell you anything about it?"

"The Path? Mrs. Quist did."

"Even better," said Belle. "She's a charter member. So you should know that according to the prophet there's not supposed to be any messing around outside wedlock."

I nodded thoughtfully. "I'm beginning to see Mr. Hoffman's problem."

"It's really low comedy in a way," said Belle. "Kalos was just pushing that dopey kid's career, that's all. He never wanted her to take off on this tangent. Because Lou's wife is one of the all-time great Believers, and she's not buying any divorce nonsense. As far as she's concerned, lover boy has just rambled off The Path under an evil spell, and she'll sit tight until he rambles back on. Kalos seconds the motion. Lou says none of this applies, because he's not a Believer anymore. But of course his wife is and his girl friend is."

I said, "You've lost me again. You say Holly Lee is a Believer. So she's holding to The Path. But she's living with Hoffman."

"Separate beds," snapped Rountree, as if this should be obvious.

57

"Well"—Belle studied her fingernails—"somehow I feel that when Lou starts climbing the walls Holly Lee yields the issue. Who knows? Maybe she gets absolution afterward."

Rountree said ponderously, "There is no absolution from leaving The Path."

"Ah, look," Belle said to him, "that girl is no Sharon Bauer. If she makes it at all, it's because of what Lou can do for her. And that's how she's playing her cards."

Rountree said with heat, "And that part of it doesn't make her any less a Believer. You know most of Kalos' followers have this—this need for material success. He encourages it. He uses it to make converts to what is really a strongly moral way of life. It wouldn't hurt you to acknowledge that much at least."

"Uh-huh," said Belle. Then she said to me, "So just remember, Mr. Milano, that when you look at cutesy Miss Otis you are looking at one of the world's great theological cockteasers."

Rountree was furious. "You really don't know any limit, do you?" He stood up and shoved her chair. "Let's go. There's almost twenty pages of script to work over."

Belle got to her feet. She said to me with forced humor, "I'm not only the bane of his life, I'm his typist and ashtray cleaner. We'll see you around, no doubt."

"No doubt. Will Kightlinger and Calderon show up here for breakfast?"

She shook her head. "Mr. K. takes breakfast in his apartment with the *Wall Street Journal*. Sometimes *Daily Variety*. Mr. Calderon will roll out of bed about one o'clock for lunch and tennis."

I said, "You mean he gets up for those sunrise services and then gets back into bed?"

Belle said chidingly, "And you a big-city boy. You caught him on the way in. He covers the clubs uptown every night until they lock up. Wine, women, song, and autographs."

I said, "Then I'll just have to catch him between shows."

"Sooner or later," said Belle. "Oh, yes. When you do

there's a question you might ask him. No, make that two questions. Why he was so hot to do this picture. And why he'd like to see the prophet Daskalos drop dead tomorrow at midnight. To put it politely."

"All right." I said. "Why?"

"He's the one to ask," said Belle.

There was a matching pair of guards at the entrance to the Annex, both of them heavyset, swarthy, and cold-eyed, with guns strapped on outside their uniform jackets. One of them led me by way of a gargantuan gym and a labyrinth of steam rooms and rubdown rooms to a pool which could have floated a fairsized yacht.

Quist, naked, was swimming in the pool, using only arm and shoulder power, legs trailing. A man in trunks stood by, keeping an eye on him. Spotting me, Quist held on to the edge of the pool for support and invited me in for a swim. I put up a mild argument against it and lost. When I joined him for a couple of lazy turns back and forth he said, "How about a little race?"

"I'm afraid I'm not that much of a swimmer."

"From the look of it, you're lying. One hundred dollars. You can use a diving start."

I said, "Make it one dollar, and we'll start even."

"One dollar it is." Then, as if reading my mind, "And you'd better do your damnedest, John. If you don't, I'll know it."

I didn't do my damnedest at first. Then he looked back over his shoulder and yelled, "Move, you bastard!" so I did. To my surprise he beat me by several lengths, easily making up on the straightways what I gained on the turns. Bracing himself on the pool's edge as he watched me come in blowing hard, he looked as jubilant as any kid who ever hit a winning homer in playground ball. He said, "Now how about a return match?" and I had just enough wind left to refuse the offer with thanks.

We adjourned to a steam room. The attendant helped

plant Quist on a tiled shelf and seemed glad to get away, closing the door behind him. Sitting there in that fog swathed in a bath sheet, Quist looked more than ever like a Roman senator. A drop of sweat trickled down his nose, and he thrust out his lower lip to blow it away. He said, "When Virgilio told me he'd guarantee competent replacements for the regular staff these few days I should have realized he meant competent in the Cuban sense of the word. On the other hand, we can at least count on tight-shut mouths."

I said, "What did he do, sign on his family?" and Quist looked startled. "Did he tell you that?"

"No. It was intended as a joke."

Quist said with amusement, "That's how close a joke can come to the truth. There's probably quite an aggregation of cousins and nephews on the job here, but most of these people belong to an organization he heads. Cuba Libertad. A Cuba freedom movement."

"That he did tell me about. I have to admit none of it sounded too realistic."

"It's not." Quist's bald head was running rivulets. He worked it over with a towel from the stack between us. "The second generation of emigrés aren't Cubans any more, they're Cuban-American. To them, Virgilio and his movement are history book stuff. But don't ever try to tell him that. He and his hard core have scores to settle. Most of them were at the Bay of Pigs."

"Araujo too?"

"Wounded there and held prisoner for a long time. His brother was killed there."

I said, "Talk about scores to settle. Still, his idea of putting together a private army, this time without CIA backing, and raising the millions of dollars it would take—"

"I know. A sad old Don Quixote. But he's not really counting on millions. He'd gladly settle tomorrow for, oh, say, five hundred thousand. Seed money, you might call it."

I said, "Now, what gives me the feeling he's asked you for that five hundred thousand?"

"Oh, yes. Oh, yes indeed. But I'm a businessman,

John, I might back Sancho Panza. Never Don Quixote." He held up a warning hand. "Don't get the wrong idea. Off hours, Virgilio may have his dreams of glory. On the job, as a specialist in security he's as good as you can get."

"Possibly. But so far I've seen one man on duty at the main gate, two at the door here, and that's all. I'd call that pretty thin security."

Quist said, "Because you haven't made the rounds with him yet, have you?" and when I admitted I hadn't he said, "Then you couldn't know there's a man in the boathouse keeping an eye on the beach area. And the cottage close to Daskalos' isn't really unoccupied. Since Saturday, there's always someone out of sight in there keeping close watch."

"Why out of sight? I'd say highly visible security is what's called for under these conditions."

Quist, forgetting where he was, drew a deep breath, sucking in a lungful of steam. He coughed hard, then winced. "Damn. You cough and it goes right down to the ankles." He pointed. "That's a cold-water tap. I could stand a dousing."

I filled the plastic bucket under the tap and doused him, then doused myself. It eased the pounding of the pulse in my temples a little. Quist showed no signs of heavy going at all. He said, "Visible security? Forget it."

"Just like that?"

"Daskalos doesn't want to be protected from whoever's threatening him. Saturday morning, Virgilio put a man at his door. Ten minutes later, the man reported back. It seemed Daskalos had come outside in a tearing rage, told him that God would put a curse on him if he didn't go away and stay away. A highly impressive performance. Especially to somebody who believes in that kind of God."

"And that's when you had your talk with Daskalos about clearing out?"

"Mrs. Quist spoke to him first. When she made no headway she asked me to step in." Quist slapped a hand down on the wet tile. "Incredible. Here he was, said he, and here he would stay. And no one was to get in the way of his murderer, whoever that was."

"I suppose he gave you the same fancy reincarnation line he gave me."

"At great length."

"Do you believe he means it?"

Quist cocked his head at me. "Yes." It looked and sounded like a challenge.

"But you know his record."

"More than that. I met him when he was still at his astrology racket some years ago. Corinthian Productions was having its bad spell then, it was up for grabs, and I thought it might be a good buy. I was on the West Coast involved in some useless negotiations on it for a couple of weeks, and twice Daskalos—Kondracki then—turned up at house parties I attended. A striking-looking man, very smooth, very charismatic, and obviously, to me at least, a total fake. Amazing how those people kowtowed to him."

"Amazing," I said with malice.

Quist's lips twisted into the suggestion of a smile. "I know what you mean. But that was Kondracki."

"Then he turned into Daskalos and a miracle took place."

"As for that—" Quist said. He stopped there. Then he said abruptly, "This isn't a change of subject. I want you to bear with me a moment."

"Sure."

"Well"—he seemed to be searching for the words—"when Mrs. Quist suggested—advised—that I call you down here, it was because in London you had handled a certain matter for her with complete success. What she emphasized was that to you the word confidential means confidential. In blunt language: when you deal with a client's very private concerns you know how to keep your mouth shut about them."

"It goes with the down payment," I said. Whatever he intended to reply was cut short by a painful grimace. He shifted the position of his legs with an effort. I asked, "Is there something I can do?"

"Not in the way of therapy. All I want from you is

your assurance that when you leave here you will not, under any conditions, head for some newspaper editor or book publisher. I think that what I've paid you—"

"Understood," I said.

"I hope so. Because to explain why I'm certain Daskalos believes in his peculiar calling, I'm going to risk telling you the circumstances surrounding my marriage. I was at a gathering some associates had arranged in my honor. That was in Acapulco about three years ago. Among the guests were screen star Sharon Bauer, and as her partner for the evening, Daskalos. As a matter of fact, this must have been soon after you handled that matter for her in London.

"Anyhow, I had seen her films and was very much an admirer from a distance. Now I seized the opportunity and asked for an introduction. She came over, introduced herself and—thank God there weren't any ears that close—she simply and directly proposed marriage. Drunk? Drugged? She didn't seem to be. So it had to be some kind of tasteless joke, and that's how I treated it. Until she told me with the most enchanting seriousness that, no, it wasn't a joke. That our marriage was ordained by her spiritual guide, Kalos Daskalos, and it might be best if I spoke to him about it." Quist motioned at the far wall. "That valve is the steam control. If you turn it down a bit, we can start to decompress. This heat isn't getting to you, is it?"

"Not at all," I lied. I turned the valve down more than a bit.

"Well then," Quist said. "I didn't speak to Daskalos at the time, just to this extraordinarily beautiful and very strange girl. And spent the next afternoon with her, learning that she was without doubt the most ingenuous creature on God's earth. If there was a conspiracy of some sort going on, she certainly wasn't part of it.

"But that evening I made a point of paying Daskalos a visit. Remember, I had known him as Kondracki, an astrologer who lived in Beverly Hills, drove a Rolls, dressed like a peacock. In Acapulco, he occupied a shabby little two-room flat in the native quarter— Sharon Bauer, believe it or not was settled in one of the rooms—and he gave every indication of really being some sort of pauper sage.

"I don't have to tell you, John, what he talked about in general; you got a taste of it yourself this morning. But his immediate concern was that the paths of his disciple and myself met at this exact time and place, that our marriage was foreordained, that if we entered into it now, we would find happiness for the rest of our lives."

"So you entered into it."

"Obviously. Want to know what was in my mind when I debated taking the plunge? First, that we always wind up sorriest for the things we haven't done. Second, that however it turned out, I could afford it. And if you haven't already noted the evidence, I can tell you it's turned out very well indeed."

I said, "I'm still trying to zero in on Daskalos. He must have gained something from playing matchmaker, didn't he?"

"A payment of some kind?" Quist shook his head. "Nothing at all. He never suggested it. I never offered it."

"And Mrs. Quist?"

"As a matter of fact, she once asked me that same question. It then turned out that neither of us had made any payment to Daskalos. She once used to pay Kondracki very generously for his astrological charts. She's never given Daskalos a penny. She seemed shocked by the idea."

I said, "He must have some source of income."

"Possibly. But consider that he needs almost nothing. He's settled down in San Francisco now. I understand that his quarters there are no improvement over the dismal hole I visited in Acapulco."

"On the other hand, he's living far away from San Francisco now. In very handsome style."

"Not all that handsome," Quist countered. "And only because Mrs. Quist urged this visit on him. She likes him close by on occasion. After all, she regards him as her trusted chaplain and confidant."

"With your approval?"

"With my approval." Quist eyed me narrowly. Evidently satisfied by whatever he read in my face, he said, "I'll put it very bluntly, John. My wife is an extremely childlike young woman. She also happens to be a living temptation to any conscienceless goddam male who catches sight of her. So it's a great comfort to know she has utter faith in a chaplain who demands an old-fashioned morality in his followers." He smiled thinly. "Need I be more explicit?"

"Hardly. Why did she want him here now? To help make up her mind about going back into pictures?"

"Well, the screenplay she's been offered deals with incest. And in the end no one is penalized for practicing it. Before Mrs. Quist would sign any contract she wanted Daskalos' judgment of this."

"Which was?"

"That certainly a penalty must be imposed on the sinners. That's what Kightlinger and company are at work on now. A reframing of the story to meet that requirement."

I said, "So all in all it seems that Daskalos is pretty much in charge here," and Quist frowned. "In what sense?"

I said, "He's deciding if the movie'll be made and how it'll be made. He's practically dictating security procedures to Araujo. Most of all, by staying on here despite those threats he's made you accountable for his safety. I call that being in charge."

Quist said stiffly, "On the other hand, remember it's someone else who's making the threats. I will admit that if Mr. Daskalos would pack himself off—"

"Which he can't do as long as he claims to believe the threats. It would mean blowing his credibility as a messiah itching to be a human sacrifice. Goodby, Believers. Back to the mail-order astrology charts."

Quist abstractedly scratched his chest while he weighed this. Then he said abruptly, "Well, he can't have it all his way. You're to personally provide him maximum protection under any conditions. That is the bottom line. I want you right there with him tomorrow night no matter how he objects to it."

"Or sounds as if he's objecting to it."

Quist said wearily, "Sometimes I'm not sure we're talking about the same man. Of course, the best solution would be for you to identify the mischief-maker, then close out matters in private. Maybe you ought to let it be known that I don't plan any action in response to the dog's being killed. As for my backing the film, that's Mrs. Quist's decision to make. In brief, the spirit of amnesty prevails."

"Really prevails?" I asked pleasantly. "Or do I come bearing the olive branch while you follow with the shillelagh behind your back?"

Quist chuckled. "Distrustful bastard, aren't you?" and there was a heavy banging at the door. It opened without invitation, and the attendant's head popped in. "The telephone," he said. "The lady—Miss Riley—wants Mr. Milano to please come quick to the office."

Quist said apprehensively to me, "John—" and I said, "I'm on my way."

And was.

Maggie, looking furious, was alone in her office She burst out: "Sid Kightlinger—" then took me in wonderingly. "You're dripping wet."

"And I tore my shirt getting it on, and I'm not wearing socks. Never mind that. What about Kightlinger?"

"First go upstairs and change those clothes. No, I'll get you one of Andrew's robes." She was almost out of the room when I thought to call after her, "And a drink. Emergency-sized."

She came back with a heavy terrycloth robe and a balloon glass half full of what turned out to be cognac. A very fine cognac. I took a hefty ungourmetlike belt of it, and while getting into the robe I said, "You'd better call the boss and tell him you're still in one piece. Right now he has his doubts about it."

She made the call, and when she put down the phone was on the way back to her original mood. "It was Sid Kightlinger," she said between her teeth. She pointed accusingly at the typewriter.

I looked at the typewriter. "What about him?"

"He wrote those notes. I'm sure of it."

"What makes you so sure?"

"Look, I go to the museum on business twice a week. I'm usually back by two. Today I cleared up my work fast, and I got back about fifteen minutes ago." She glanced at her watch. "That's right. Eleven-thirty."

I said, "At the rate you're telling it, I'll finish this whole crock of brandy before you're done. Then I won't remember a word of it."

"All right. Sid knows about my museum trips and when I'm usually back from them."

"And this time, since he wasn't prepared for your early return, he was caught redhanded at that typewriter."

"How'd you guess that?"

"There wasn't much else to guess. Did he ever use the machine before that you know of?"

"No."

"So you caught him in the act. What happened then?"

"Well, he looked stupefied—it's the only way to put it—then very angry. That's the paper he was using, by the way. My paper. The drawer's still open. And that envelope must have been the one he was going to use."

I said, "Interesting. He's never been in here before, but he certainly seems to know his way around."

"He has been in here. I once typed a letter for him. What I said was I never knew *him* to use the machine before. Anyhow, before I could get a look at what he was typing he snatched it out of the machine and started crumpling it up. I said: 'Kindly let me see that.' "

"In those words?"

"More or less. And he stood up and said, 'Kindly mind your own fucking business.' That's when I saw a typewriter ribbon in the wastepaper basket. I hadn't changed ribbons, so he must have. Which meant he wanted to use a fresh one just like those notes were done with. So I grabbed for the paper in his hand. And he hit me."

"Really hit you?"

"Slapped me. Full force. It hurt like hell." Like a kid inviting sympathy, she pulled aside some of that waterfall of hair to display the reddened imprint on her cheek. I also found that, freckles, snubnose and all, this was a highly pleasing girl-next-door face I was regarding close up.

I said, "So he slapped you. Then what?"

"I socked him. Hard. He'll remember it."

I said with admiration, "That's my girl," and she waited for more than that. "Well?" she finally said.

"Well, what?"

"What are you going to do about him, that's what."

I said, "You know, this kind of repartee is what helped kill vaudeville. Exactly what do you expect me to do about him?"

Maggie said in outrage, "Find out what he was writing. Give him the Frankie Kurtz treatment if you have to."

"But there was no chance Frankie Kurtz would sue me. There's every chance Kightlinger would. Along with you and Quist. And here come all those newspaper reporters Quist hates. Right?"

"Oh, is it?" Maggie said with elaborate sarcasm. "And would that worry you so much if it wasn't Kalos who was being threatened with murder?"

I said, "Hold it, tiger. Let's stick to Kightlinger. Now, what reason would he have for being our mystery man?"

"Him? Plenty of reason. From what I've heard, he's produced two losers in a row, and he needs a winner bad. And he thought he had one until Kalos came along."

"That's something to know when I talk to him. Now, I want some accurate information about what happened in Quist's office after the dog was found dead. You told me that pretty soon everyone showed up to take a look. Are you sure that included Kightlinger?"

Brow furrowed, she turned this over in her mind. "I honestly can't remember."

"Then let's view the scene of the crime. That might help."

In Quist's office I told her to stand where she had been standing when the company started to arrive, and she moved behind the desk, a fair distance from the bleached portion of the carpet. She pointed at the discoloration. "Andrew was there. And Holly Lee and Lou Hoffman and the Rountrees were across the room there. And Sharon and Mike Calderon were by that window."

"Definitely Calderon?"

"Yes. He had his arms around Sharon and was making a big thing of comforting her. I'll admit she was in a bad way."

"What about Kightlinger? Do you remember seeing him here?"

She shook her head. "No, I don't."

"Then we'll assume he wasn't. One more question. You mentioned a pool of blood around the dog. Was any of it spattered on the furniture or walls?"

She looked repelled by the idea. "No. When I had the help in to clean up, that part of the carpet was the only thing that needed cleaning. What are you getting at anyway?"

"I'm doing some heavy detecting. Cut the throat of any large, active animal, and odds are you'll wind up with a roomful of blood before it gives up struggling and dies. Unless it was heavily sedated in advance. So there's every chance Rufus was close to dead before the throat-cutting."

Maggie frowned at me. "Is that why you asked about hypodermics last night? Because someone might have used one on Rufus?"

"Yes. Now I'd say someone definitely used one. That wrecks the theory that Kightlinger didn't show up for the post mortem because he was busy getting rid of bloodstained clothing. Fact is, he could have had a dozen valid reasons for not showing up. By the way, where was Araujo at the time? You didn't number him among those present."

"Because Friday's his day at the museum setting up weekend security." She motioned toward the phone on the desk. "That's why I was standing here. Andrew told me to call him as soon as we saw what had happened. Virgilio was here about twenty minutes later. But what do you plan to do about Sid and whatever he was writing? You can't just brush that aside, can you? It could have been one of those notes."

I said, "It's almost noon. What's the lunch schedule here?" and Maggie answered, "Buffet, noon to two. Dinner's at eight. Irish linen napkins and wear a jacket."

"I have the jacket but I'm starting to run out of shirts. Anyhow, I'd like to catch Kightlinger before he comes down to lunch. If he comes down. How's the cheek, by the way? Cooling a little?"

"A little."

I said on mischievous impulse, "Suppose I offer to kiss it and make it better?"

She actually backed away a step, looking panicky. "Wrong room, doctor," she said. "Wrong patient."

So far.

Following the sound old rule of waste not, want not, I took the balloon glass back to my apartment—there was enough left to easily see me through the next thirty-six hours—and once again got myself ready to meet company. When I knocked on Kightlinger's door, however, there was no answer, and when I looked into the apartment, a duplicate of mine down to the lingering smell of wood smoke in the air, there was no one at home.

I went back to my quarters, checked through the Hesperides phone directory and called valet service. Eventually, the beautiful Pablo showed up. He looked over yesterday's wilted shirt and this morning's shirt minus a button and assured me that both would be made ready for me to wear in a couple of hours. Anything else?

I said, "Just a question. Is there an automated switchboard for the phones here, or is somebody supposed to be sitting at it?"

"Somebody's supposed to be at it all the time."

"One more question. How do I borrow or rent a car if I want to do a little sightseeing?"

"The garage'll fix you up." Pablo picked up the phone. "Chauffeur or plain?"

"Plain," I said, and Pablo, after making the call, reported: "It'll be around in five minutes. Only thing is, when you get back, park it at the garage. A sharp right inside the gate and just keep going. They'll drive you to the house here."

He departed with my shirts and ten tax-free dollars, and I made a close study of the Miami area map. Then

I went outside to find that plain meant a neat little Toyota wagon. I stopped at the main gate for inspection, turned south on Old Cutler Road, which led me to U.S. 1, where I turned north. Just as the map had indicated, I passed the Serpentarium, and just as I had estimated, I came to a shopping center not far beyond it.

In a drug and sundries store plus lunch counter were phone booths. I charged the call to the agency, and Shirley Glass cut short my friendly hello by remarking with satisfaction: "The weatherman said this morning you were having a real bad cold wave down there." She clicked her tongue in false sympathy.

I said, "I don't know where those guys get their ideas. It's eighty degrees and not a cloud in the sky. Any significant messages?"

"Your sister Angie, bright and early. And that Elphinstone from the insurance company. I turned him over to Willie."

"What'd Mr. Elphinstone have on his well-bred mind?"

"According to Willie, he thinks there's a leak somewhere in his office. He wants a plant in there to track it down."

"I figured he'd get around to that. Now I want you to do a job for me. Top priority. There's that movie gossip female on TV. Her leg man—you know who I mean—owes us a big one."

"McNulty. Owen McNulty."

"Right. Get through to him on the Coast. Tell him I want whatever he's got on any connection between Michael Calderon and somebody who calls himself Kalos Daskalos. Also known as Walter Kondracki." I spelled out the names for her. "And don't let Willie in on this because he'll start arguing price with McNulty. You handle it yourself."

Shirley said, "Can do. Say, that's the movie Mike Calderon, isn't it? Is he there with you?"

"Not me exclusively. Now, understand this. I want that information, if any, by five this afternoon. I'll phone you then."

"Okay. And getting to the interesting part, how is the divine Mrs. Quist?"

I said, "Right here in bed with me. Want to say hello to her?" and Shirley, after a quick count, said, "You think I think you're kidding, Johnny, but I'm not so sure." She hung up on that.

I went over to the lunch counter and had a b.l.t. on soggy toast and an earful of talk about the weather from some unhappy locals. Then, reversing my course, I drove to the Serpentarium and put in time there, making the rounds of the reptile world and winding up watching the man in charge extract venom from several edgy snakes.

It struck me on the way out that he and I had a lot more in common than anyone might suspect at first glance.

As requested, I returned the car to the garage, and considering the dimensions of everything else here at the top of the beanstalk it was no surprise to find that the garage was a block long, two-story fieldstone capable of servicing a couple of dozen cars.

Araujo was outside, clipboard in hand, laying down the law to some uniformed men. I surrendered the wagon to a mechanic and walked over to him. He introduced me to his second-in-command, didn't bother about an introduction to the others. Then, a hand planted between my shoulder blades, he steered me toward the building. "I've been waiting to show you around," he said. Out of earshot of the others, he confided, "I just had a talk with the boss. It seems you weren't too happy about the security here."

"Well, that may have been a snap judgment."

"Mr. Quist didn't think so." Araujo was surprisingly full of good cheer about it. "You managed to convince him we're shorthanded in our security. Up to now, I couldn't."

When I asked why not he held out a hand and rubbed thumb and fingers together meaningfully. "Call it economy. But now we'll be doing it the way it should be done. Including around-the-clock patrols. And closed-circuit monitoring by next week."

He led me up a flight of narrow stairs to show me his command post, a small room with a man at a desk on which were a couple of phones and walkie-talkie. On the wall were a large map of the estate, divided into grids, and a blowup of Maggie's plan of the main building. The rest of these rooms above the garage, Araujo

76

said, waving in their direction, were bedrooms, sixteen of them. Two for the family's chauffeurs, the rest for the chauffeurs of visitors. He explained: "We do some stylish entertaining now and then. Last Christmas there were eighty guests here for the week."

"Some economy," I said.

He gave me a gold-toothed smile. "And champagne and caviar by the truckload. But God help you"—he raised his eyes to heaven—"if one spoon was missing afterward. One lousy towel. Did you happen to notice that there are no pictures in your apartment?"

"I did."

"The result of that Christmas celebration. There used to be reproductions of art works in every room. Department-store stuff. Then some guest for a joke—after all, what the hell are those things worth?—took one with him when he left. Smuggled it out. Next week, Mr. Quist had every picture in the guest rooms removed and stored away. The most generous of hosts, understand. But he wants it known that he'll provide the hospitality, you will not help yourself to it."

"What happened to the guest who took the picture?" I asked. Araujo answered succinctly, "Another candidate for the shit list."

We went downstairs, and he disappeared into the garage to come out in a gold cart. In it, we headed southward on a quick tour of inspection, our first stop a service building largely given over to maintenance and repair shops and to laundering equipment. Its rear section was sealed off by a wire partition. Behind the partition I made out a fair-sized generator. Generally good power service in these parts, Araujo assured me, but the auxiliary generator was always kept at the ready. A young man sat behind the partition, his uniform jacket draped over the back of his chair. When Araujo glared at him the young man hastily got into the jacket.

We mounted the golf cart again, followed the southern wall of the grounds past an empty pool fringed with cabanas and held course as far as the grassy bluff overlooking the beach where the wall ended. Here we turned northward past the Rountree cottage, past the Hoffman–Holly Lee cottage. On the tennis courts nearby Holly Lee and Calderon were playing a pat-a-ball match against Scott Rountree and Lou Hoffman. Beauty and the Beast against Mutt and Jeff.

Araujo was intrigued by the sight. "Interesting. Over the weekend they were giving each other a lot of room. Highly distrustful, you might say, after the dog was killed. Now here they are, coming together again."

"Excluding Kightlinger," I said, and Araujo said, "That's true. You've met him?"

"Not yet."

"I'd like to know what comes of it when you do. That business of his using Miss Riley's typewriter. And his violent reaction to being discovered at it. I distrust all four of those men, but I distrust him just a little more than the others."

"I see you're still being chivalrous about the ladies."

Araujo looked speculative. "Well, I've considered your idea that one of them might be involved. I think Mrs. Rountree could have that kind of disposition. I'm sure the girl hasn't."

"Some natural bias there?"

"Because she's young and pretty?" Araujo grinned. "Of course. But seriously, she's so much devoted to Mr. Daskalos it's hard to imagine her wanting to hurt him in any way."

"To test him maybe? To see if he really can deliver the goods after he's dead?"

"You're joking," Araujo said warily.

"I don't know. We're dealing with some strange people here."

He slowed the cart passing Daskalos' cottage and regarded it glumly. "The heart of our little problem."

"Did Mr. Quist give you my analysis of the problem?"

"Yes. Also word that if you can't nail the perpetrator in advance, you're supposed to play nursemaid to Mr. Daskalos tomorrow night. By the way, you do have a gun with you?"

"I'm not much on guns. I'll settle for the nursemaid part."

"Oh?" He gave me a wicked look. "And I thought you were all for highly visible security."

"*Touché.*"

"Hell." He dug a friendly elbow into my ribs. "If you change your mind, I'll fix you up with something suitable. Anyhow, that's the easy part of it."

"What's the hard part?"

"Playing nursemaid in there"—he waggled a thumb at the cottage—"without the gentleman throwing a fit. No problem if he's the swindler you think he is. A very large problem if he's the fanatic I think he is."

"And," I said, "if I do nail the perpetrator in advance, we never will know which of us is right, will we?"

Back in my pictureless apartment, I lowered the brandy level of the balloon glass another fraction of an inch, then set off down the hallway to check on Kightlinger again. Halfway to his door I was struck by inspiration. I went back to my rooms and put in a call to Maggie. After some confused going-ons by the warm body at the switchboard I was connected with her. I said, "If you're not in your office, where are you?"

"In Andrew's. With him. What is it? Did you talk to Sid Kightlinger?"

"Nor yet. Have you used that typewriter since he did?"

"No."

"Then I'll be in your office right away. You be there too. If the boss wants to come along, bring him."

They were both waiting when I got there. I said without preliminary, "If Kightlinger didn't get too far along with his typing before he was interrupted, there's a chance we can find out what he wrote without even seeing the paper."

Quist caught on fast. "The ribbon," he said, and Maggie looked at him, then at me. "I don't understand."

I explained. "A fresh ribbon can show what was typed on it before it starts respooling. After that, you'd be going over what you already wrote and blocking it out. Now, let's take a look."

I sat down at the machine, lifted out the ribbon, and unspooled it to arm's length. I scanned it closely. "Good news and bad news. The good news is that it's legible. The bad news is that this isn't any death threat."

I nodded at Maggie. "I'll read it to you. Get yourself a pencil and pad and take it down."

Jan. 17th

Dr. Jack Newstone
Medical Arts Group Building
Denver, Col.

Dear Jack:
Your check for the $2000 just arrived. As per our phone talk this letter serves as a binding agreement that your 2000 gives you 5% of my producer's share of *Two Plus One*. I will send the formal papers as soon as I am back at the office. I am very grateful to you, Jack. As to why I could not just go to Quist and ask him for some ready money there are

Maggie waited with pencil poised. "That's it?"

"That's it," I said.

Quist's face was a study. "The double-talking bastard. He's working on nickels and dimes." He didn't seem displeased about it.

I said to him, "Now we've both got leverage." I spooled the ribbon tight and put it in my pocket. "But it must be understood that for the time being neither you nor Miss Riley knows anything about this. Only I do."

Quist gave me a nod and a wink. "Naturally, it's your own little secret. For the time being."

Maggie said, "I still don't understand. What leverage? If this isn't a note to Kalos—"

I cut in: "Take a deep breath and listen. From Mr. Quist's angle, when someone wants to sell you an interest in a million-dollar deal and you suddenly find he's working on all nerve and no cash, you have him, in the fine old expression, by the balls. From my angle, if I show Kightlinger evidence that he's working on all nerve and no cash—and let him know I'll keep it quiet only if he opens up to me—well, you can see where I have him."

She could. And from the look of her she relished the

thought. She said, "You have a real mean streak, don't you?" and I said, "Same as your friend Sid. Now I'll go demonstrate it to him."

"I'd wish you luck," Quist said, "except that I never knew anyone holding a royal flush who needed it."

In the hallway Maggie said to me, "But that letter does make it look more than ever like Sid, doesn't it? If he's so broke, and Kalos stands in the way of making the movie, he has one hell of a motive to get rid of him. And you seem to be very strong on motive."

"I am. Except where the suspect is certifiably loony. But there are still some other motives around here to be explored before we clap the cuffs on Sid. Remember, a wrong guess gives the real troublemaker a clear track."

"I suppose." She touched her fingers to the injured cheek. "And even if Sid isn't the one," she said pleasurably, "I can see what'll happen now when he sits down to talk contract with Andrew."

"And with you standing there, whip in hand. Tell me something. Does Quist really operate his billion-dollar conglomerate out of his office here? My picture of how conglomerates are run—"

"Your picture's probably right. Andrew still rates chairman of the board, but he hasn't had much to do with Quistco for a few years now. Not since the pain set in bad. He felt that vital decisions made under pain or even mild sedation could easily be the wrong decisions. He's that kind of man."

"So this movie deal would be sort of a hobby for him."

Maggie shook her head. "Not if Sharon gives him the go-ahead on it. Then it becomes very serious business. Sharon's his hobby. And whatever else you want to call it. Twenty-four hours a day."

"Where is she now, come to think of it? I haven't seen her around since this morning."

Maggie said, "I was wondering when you'd ask. She's probably wondering too. She's in her bedroom allegedly having a headache. Actually having the weeps."

"Much of that lately?"

"Yes," said Maggie. She was looking at me steadily.

"Is Quist aware of it?"

"No."

The silence between us started to ring in my ears.

"Well," I said, "we all have our troubles, don't we? Now I'll go see how much I can add to Sid Kightlinger's."

This time Kightlinger was in, all Gucci and Pucci and monogrammed shirt. In the middle forties, to give him the best of it, tall, running to fat, and with a TV newscaster's super-hairstyling. When I introduced myself he said, "The house dick. I know," and stood in the doorway barring my entrance.

I suggested we'd do better in the privacy of the apartment, and he said, "We can take care of our business right here. You ask me if I'm the crackpot out to get Daskalos and I say no. That settles it. Goodby."

He started to close the door against me. I said, "Fact is, what I wanted to ask about was a Jack Newstone. Dr. Jack Newstone. Of Denver, Colorado."

Kightlinger said explosively, "That bitch!" Then, as if alarmed by his own vehemence, he peered furtively up and down the empty hallway. He motioned me in and closed the door behind us. His red-faced anger, as I watched, became red-faced confusion. "But she never saw the letter. How did she—?"

"She didn't. I'm the one." I took out the ribbon and unspooled a length of it. I held it up in demonstration. "A brand-new tattletale ribbon. Want me to read it to you?"

"Don't strain yourself." He was cautiously appraising me. "Does she know about this? Or Quist?"

I said, "Not yet," and he looked a little relieved but still on guard. I asked, "What made you change the ribbon anyhow?"

"Because why the hell shouldn't I? The other one was all used up when I tried it. It was no big deal except for that broad coming on like a storm trooper. I

84

was going to tell her I used the machine next time I ran into her."

"You belted her pretty hard considering it was no big deal."

"Because she came at me like a goddam wildcat. What was I supposed to do, run around the room with her chasing me? And she belted me pretty fucking hard too." He ran his fintertips along his jaw in pained reminiscence. "I think she cracked a couple of caps."

"I wouldn't bill Quist for them if I were you. Better to sell five percent of yourself to your dentist." I sat down on the couch and stretched out my legs to indicate I was in a mood for friendly chitchat. "How much of that producer's share have you sold already?"

"What the hell is that your business?"

"Well now, suppose I took it into my head that because you're up against the wall financially, and Daskalos is nailing you to it even tighter, you'd do anything to get rid of him?"

"Crap."

"In that case, I'll do you the favor of telling Quist you didn't kill his pet hound. That the note you were caught typing was simply thanks to a buddy for some pocket money you needed to keep up the big front. Quist would like that. After all, what wheeler-dealer doesn't like to see the party of the second part get down on his knees when it comes time to talk contract?"

Kightlinger seated himself heavily. He ran his hands up and down his thighs while he did some hard thinking. Then he said, "And what would you like? A little piece of my action just to keep your mouth shut?"

"I'm tempted, but no thanks. Is that what's going on between you and Daskalos? You offered him a little piece of your action if he okayed the movie deal, and he's holding out for more?"

Kightlinger said wearily, "He's not holding out for anything. He just turned me down cold."

"Playing hard to get?"

"I don't think so. He just turned me down, that's all. I think he's as crazy as he looks." Kightlinger held up a warning hand. "Which does not mean I'm stupid enough to try knocking him off."

"Well, someone around here seems to be. Any idea who?"

"Maybe yes, maybe no." He gnawed a hangnail. "Look, I know about you. When Bauer said you were coming down here she also let it out that you were the guy who took care of Frankie Kurtz for her. You know. After she cut loose from him but he wouldn't let go. So I got on the blower with Ted Freitag at Corinthian and asked about it. He said it was true, you were the one. And that you were very tough, but, far as he knew, strictly on the level."

I said, "A contented client is our best advertisement."

"We can skip the comedy. Freitag also told me something strictly between us. That it was Daskalos who pressured Bauer to dump Frankie Kurtz. Did you know that?"

"No. But what's it got to do with these threats against Daskalos?"

"Because Frankie Kurtz does know it. And he is only twenty minutes away from here right now. Right up there in Miami Beach."

"Visiting?"

Kightlinger said with satisfaction, "Settled in there for over a year now. Loan-sharking, they tell me."

"Who's they?"

"Some local movie union guys I'm dealing with. But here he is, only twenty minutes away. Think that over."

I thought it over. "Nope, it doesn't fit."

"Why not? Who'd have better reason than Frankie for wanting to slice Daskalos into little pieces? Do you know what it cost him when Bauer gave him the goodby?"

"Even so, it has to be an inside job."

Kightlinger said impatiently, "So he lined up one of these shmucks who works around the place here. He's loan-sharking, remember? There's other ways of paying off your loan shark than with cash. Like doing him a very large favor, for instance."

"Talking out of experience?" I said, and Kightlinger

glowered. "What is this? You just won't be happy unless you make me your fall guy?"

"Well, let's put it this way. Maggie Riley would be very happy if I made you my fall guy."

"Oho. You mean you've got a hard-on for Miss Freckles. And just because I handed her what's coming to her—"

I stood up. "It's been nice meeting you," I said as I moved toward the door, and Kightlinger came to his feet almost passionately conciliatory. "For chrissake, Milano, how about you cool it off and be reasonable? You want me to say it, all right I'll say it. I'm sorry I walloped her. But I'm right on the edge of the cliff now. If you understood my position—"

I took my time sitting down again. "All you have to do is tell me about it."

"If I can believe that's as far as it goes."

I said, "Cross my heart. You can start by telling me how come you picked Sharon Bauer for a part in your movie. I mean, knowing she was supposed to be retired from the business. Was that your brainstorm, or did she send up signals?"

"Neither. Not exactly. Look. Let me lay it out in one piece so you'll get the whole picture."

"Without embroidery."

Kightlinger held up both hands placatingly. "The straight goods. What happened was I came across this book *Two Plus One* a couple of years ago, and I could see it had possibilities. You know anything about screen production?"

"I did jobs for some of Freitag's problem people. Mostly the ones marked self-destruct. That's as far as it goes."

"Then I have to explain that when it comes to a small independent like me you can't compete with the big boys for hot properties. You settle for what's available, and it turned out this book was. So I settled with Rountree for rights to the book and a screenplay. He did a good job on the screenplay for the first time out. Not perfect, but very good. So I'm in business. Now what's needed is financing and a release—a guarantee of distribution, y'understand—but when I go to the major studios they all turn me down."

"The incest problem?"

"Nah, incest is in right now. It's just that what I offered was a people picture, and today it's all spectaculars. Go to a major with a solid story about just people—live human beings, y'understand—hand them a budget for two million, they die laughing. Tell them you've got a story about how the Empire State Building falls down on Central Park and lets loose all the lions in the zoo and they run around town killing people, and they ask if you'll be happy with twenty million. Thirty million. You name it."

I said, "It wouldn't land on Central Park."

"What?"

"The Empire State's on Thirty-fourth Street. If it fell down, it wouldn't reach Central Park. The park's on Sixtieth."

"Oh, for chrissake, you know what I mean. Did you happen to read Rountree's book, by the way?"

"No."

"It's worth reading. There's this brother and sister. He's straight animal. She's very sensual, y'understand, but innocent. When they're kids there's always electricity between them. Then he marries himself a very young girl who's crazy about him, sort of a duplicate of his sister. But it's no use. He and the sister are drawn together like a couple of mink sniffing each other out. Then there are circumstances one weekend—"

"Let's omit the circumstances."

"All right, so the brother and sister wind up in bed together. It sets off an affair they keep fighting against and losing. The young wife feels something's wrong, but can't believe her own suspicions. When the showdown comes it's too much for her. She kills herself. And the finish is her burial, the brother and sister standing together at her grave while the dirt is being dumped into it. And what do we see close up? He tries to put an arm around her, she resists, he wins. And, baby, when she leans against him it's plain to one and all that they now

have exactly what they really wanted from the start."
Kightlinger's eyes were bright with enthusiasm. "Well,
what do you think?"

"Not bad. Except from what I heard, Daskalos ruled
that your sinners can't live happily ever after. Which
means some big changes in the script. Did I hear
wrong?"

Kightlinger said bitterly, "No, you did not hear
wrong. That fucking Daskalos is a disease."

"How does Rountree feel about making those
changes?"

"Well, he kind of goes for Daskalos' line, so he's
being smart about it. It's his big-mouth wife who's making the trouble."

"She his artistic conscience?"

"Whatever you want to call it. Anyhow, she ought to
know by now that if it ain't Freitag and Corinthian, it's
nobody."

I said, "How did it get to be Freitag in the first
place?"

Kightlinger almost smiled. "You wouldn't believe
how that happened. First time around he turned the
story down flat. But I had a feeling he was kind of
hooked by it. So I kept coming back to him until all of
a sudden he says—maybe it was supposed to be a gag,
but what the hell—anyhow, he says, 'You get Mike
Calderon and Sharon Bauer together again for this one,
and Corinthian'll go for fifty percent. And a release.'
And, God damn it, I went out and got him Mike Calderon just like that."

"How? I read somewhere he gets at least a million off
the top. On your kind of budget—"

Kightlinger said, "He gets a million from somebody
else. From me it'll be deferred money and a big chunk
of the gross. Why? Because Bauer is the one piece he
made a picture with he couldn't get into. The one and
only where she didn't lay down and spread her legs
when he told her to. It really eats him, not scoring with
her. And here's one more chance to do it."

I said, "You sold him the deal on that basis?" and

Kightlinger answered reproachfully, "Do I look like another Frankie Kurtz? I gave him the script, that's all. And I kind of convinced him that Bauer was set to play the sister. And when I finally got through to her she didn't seem to mind at all it would be Mike."

"I see. And how did Lou Hoffman get himself picked as director?"

"He's Mike's pick. He worked with Mike, he knows how Mike likes things done. And Holly Lee is Lou's pick."

I said, "There seems to be a lot of incest going on outside of that script," and Kightlinger gave me a wise smile. "In my position, Milano, that's how you do it. If you know how." The smile faded. "Except that I am mortgaged up to the fucking eyeballs. And just when I'm ready to strike oil, along comes this craziness with those notes and that mutt getting killed. My only hope is that it all turns out to be a big nothing."

"Suppose it turns out to be a big something?"

"Then it has got to be Frankie Kurtz. Vendetta stuff, know what I mean? So if you could wrap him up until I'm all set here—"

I cut in: "Even if I could, I wouldn't. I know Kurtz. Money is his game, not three-year-old vendettas. If one of those notes was an extortion note, that might earmark him. None of them was."

Kightlinger once more attacked the hangnail with his teeth. Finally he said, "If it's not him—"

"Yes?"

"Nothing. Talking to myself."

"It sounded like you were getting around to something interesting."

"Ah, look. You have got to be reasonable, Milano. I come out with the wrong name, next thing on top of all my other troubles I get hit with a libel suit."

"Slander."

"Huh?"

I said, "Libel is when you put it in writing. Slander is when you say it. And I'm the only one around to hear you say it."

"I already said enough. Anyhow, if I were you I'd

take it easy on this job. If it's not Frankie Kurtz, then it's someone right here. And just having you around, you know what I mean, should cool off whoever it is."

"There's always that," I said.

"I know that part. Just stick to the connection between him and Calderon."

This time when I phoned the garage it was a Mercedes 280 that was brought around. I hadn't allowed for the going-home traffic that would start clogging the roads at five o'clock, so I was in the phone booth at the shopping center about fifteen minutes behind schedule.

Shirley simply called this to my attention. Then she said, "Sometimes I honest-to-God sympathize with Angie. I don't know what's going on down there, and when you don't call on time—"

She sounded so upset that I put aside the impulse to tell her that an Italian big sister, an Italian mother, and a self-elected Jewish mother were too much of a load altogether. I said, "Nothing's happening down here. It's a gas."

"Oh? Still in bed with Mrs. Quist?"

"No, I wore her out. I'm taking a turn with her husband's secretary now. A real doll. Come on, Shirl, were you able to reach what's-his-name?"

"Owen McNulty. Yes."

"Did he know of any connection between Calderon and Daskalos?"

"He did. And it must be good too, because it's costing us five hundred. McNulty says, please, no agency check. It has to be a cashier's check."

"Any way he wants it. What's his story?"

"Well, this Daskalos runs some kind of weird little religious organization—you know, California style—with mostly film and TV people in it. About a hundred of them. But he used to be—"

"I know that part. Just stick to the connection between him and Calderon."

"All right. Calderon's wife is really the one with the connection. His present wife. Now I have to give you some background, whether you like it or not."

"Mrs. Calderon's?"

"Just listen. Calderon's first three wives were all glamour girls who had no children. McNulty says this number four is a pretty little nobody who was always being kept out of sight while Calderon went his merry way. But she did have a child by him. Michael Junior. Now six years old. Are you with me?"

"Yes."

"Good. Now here's where McNulty says he doesn't have all he needs to break the story, but enough to make his theory about it look very strong. From what he's put together, he believes Mrs. Calderon came under the influence of this Daskalos. And Daskalos convinced her that she couldn't go on living with a totally adulterous husband. So a couple of months ago she went off with the child to her parents' home in Seattle and hasn't come back to Calderon since."

I said, "How far did McNulty push this?"

"He went up to the Seattle house, he saw the child playing in the yard, but he says the place is guarded like Fort Apache by some real goons. Then he hunted up Daskalos, who told him that he was under an evil spell and to go get lost. He finally put the question right to Calderon, and he feels he was close to getting murdered on the spot. He says he didn't push it any further because it's not that big a story, especially since this is wife number four and a nobody. I think he convinced himself it's not that big a story."

I said, "But he believes Daskalos did bust up Calderon's marriage."

"Well, the marriage seems to be the least part of it. McNulty says it's possible Calderon doesn't even remember his wife's name. But losing his one and only child—a son at that—might hurt bad. It's hard to tell with somebody like Calderon. And that's your five-hundred-dollar's worth, Johnny. Say, are you still there?"

"Yes."

"Nice to know. I thought I put you to sleep with all this."

"Far from it," I said.

T he sky to the east was just starting to darken when I got back to the garage. I went upstairs to security headquarters, where Araujo's second-in-command greeted me respectfully, and in answer to my query, explained that, no, there was no going home for any staff or security people this week; everyone on duty understood he had signed on for full-time residence here until Saturday. Mr. Araujo had insisted on that.

I said, "So there's no chance any of them could make personal contact with someone on the outside?"

"By phone, yes. Otherwise no."

"How about deliveries coming in?"

"I supervise them myself. The driver isn't permitted to leave the truck."

I said, "It's almost like combat duty, isn't it?" and he said cheerfully, "Yes, it is. But much more comfortable."

A mechanic dropped me off at the entrance to the main building. As he pulled away, Sharon and Maggie came outside all done up for cool weather. I said to them, "Time for sunset services?"

Sharon nodded. Her eyes, making contact with mine, were wide with appeal. Maggie said, "Did you talk to Sid?"

"I did. I wouldn't swear to it, but he seemed ready to finger somebody here. Then he suddenly clammed up. Which is understandable. Send any of his package away in disgrace, and the game is all over for him."

"But didn't Andrew tell you that if whoever it is admits it, he's ready to forgive and forget? If Sid knew that—"

"He wouldn't believe it. For that matter, neither do I."

"Because you don't know Andrew." She looked disappointed. "So that's all it came to with Sid."

"Well, he's sorry he hit you, if you want to buy that. On the other hand, he thinks you cracked some of his caps."

"Good."

"I knew that would brighten your day." Then, honestly curious, I asked, "Why do you attend these services? Working up to a conversion?"

"Hardly. But no matter how you feel about it, Milano, they do help ease the troubled spirit." She seemed embarrassed by the confession. "Maybe any ritual like that would."

"Maybe. I'll leave you two ladies to it, then."

I was poised for departure, but Sharon suddenly brought me to heel. "Johnny, wait." She turned to Maggie. "You go on alone."

Maggie hesitated. Then gave me a warning look which did everything but shout "You be nice to this child, hear?" and with a flip of the hand went her way beachward. She cut a fine figure with that full-legged stride.

Sharon said to me, "You like her, don't you?"

"Yes."

"A lot?"

I said, "If what's on your mind is how I feel about Miss Riley—"

"No. Let's go inside."

One of the rooms off the transverse corridor beside the elevator was a mini-theater with a pitched floor and rows of armchairs descending from the projectionist's booth to the screen down front. Sharon seated herself against the back wall and huddled into her coat. I took the chair beside hers. She sat staring at the blank screen, and then her hand found mine and gripped it tightly. She said to the screen: "When you go back to New York I want to go with you."

I said, "We can talk about anything but that. Like, for instance, this handsome little showplace. What kind of film does Andrew go for? Regular showings of *Patton*?"

"No. Just mine. He likes to be here with me and watch them. They turn him on."

"And so to bed?"

"Yes."

"But there's nothing porno about those films."

"I know."

I said, "Well, that's another one for the sex instruction books. On the other hand, I can't fault him. He's managed to achieve what a large part of our male population can only dream of."

Now she looked at me. "I wish you wouldn't talk like that. I said it turns him on. It doesn't turn me on. It makes me sick."

"His loving attentions?"

"No, not that. The whole scene. I mean, he gets himself all horny watching me up there, but it's not really me. And I'm watching myself and I hate it. I always hated to even look at the rushes when I was making the pictures."

"Why? The way you come across on the screen—"

"But I'm not an actress, don't you understand? An *actress* actress. I don't know how to do it, I just do it. So I was scared all the time on the set. And when I sit here watching I'm scared all over again, remembering how it felt."

I said, "It doesn't mean anything to you that you always manage to do it right? That even someone as tough as Pauline Kael wrote that you were one of the great screen naturals?"

"I know all that. It doesn't mean anything."

"In that case, why the hell did you decide to go back into pictures?"

"Because it got so that I had to do something. What else could I do except go back into pictures? But if you would only—"

"No. You could do what other women in your position do."

Sharon said bitterly, "Shopping. And backgammon. And tennis. And traveling. And screwing around with the local studs. And more shopping. I don't give a fuck about any of that."

I said in resignation, "All right, I can see we'll have to settle for your choice of subject. You plan to make a movie. What happens to the movie if you go back to New York with me?"

"Who cares? That's Sid's problem."

"I guess it is. But there's something else. What about your guru's high moral standards? I hear he's already got Lou Hoffman and his girl operating on some kind of weird separate-beds basis. Is that what you see for us until the divorce comes through?"

Sharon said huskily, "Oh, no. Not a chance."

"Then you agree with me about Daskalos?"

She shook her head. "I didn't say that. I just can't be a Believer any more, that's all. It doesn't work for me."

"Moving in with me wouldn't work either."

"Yes, it would. You already found out it would."

"Because of those two weeks we had? Under what might be called highly unreal conditions? No. I've had plenty of time to consider those two weeks and what they really came to. You had twenty-three years of talk bottled up in you, and you finally had a chance to let it all out. And probably for the first time in your life you were with someone who didn't want to exploit you in any way. Who only wanted you to enjoy life, because when you did he did. Therapy, that's what it was. And when you'd gotten all you could out of the treatment you signed on with another specialist."

"No. That part of it isn't true. Why didn't you read those letters I sent you? It's all there." She tugged my hand. "If I gave them to you now, would you read them?"

I said, "You keep them around here? Let me tell you out of professional experience, lady, that is extremely foolish of you."

"You don't have to be a detective all the time. Maggie's got them locked up with her own personal things. Will you read them?"

"There's no point to it. It won't change anything."

98

"Please."

That magical, murderous please. I struck my colors but refused to scuttle the ship. "All right, I'll read them. On one condition. We drop the subject now and stick to cases. Notably the case your husband's paying me to handle for him."

She squeezed my hand hard. "Yes. What about the case?"

"A question. And there'd better be a truthful answer. Has Frankie Kurtz been in touch with you since London?"

"No."

"Do you know where he is right now?"

"I suppose on the Coast."

I said, "Right here. Miami Beach for the past year. Probably gotten himself into the papers too, now and then. And you had no idea of that?"

"I don't read the papers much." Her voice became apprehensive. "Johnny, do you think he's the one?"

"Not if he hasn't sent you any threats or demands. Just remember that if he does, you let Quist know about it right away. Never fall for that line about keeping it quiet or else."

"Yes. But I'd rather tell you about it if it happens."

I said pointedly, "Except that I won't be here to tell."

That silenced her for a short count. Then she said, "What do you think's going to happen tomorrow night?"

"I'm not sure. Odds are nothing'll happen. Not under the conditions that prevail."

"Because you're here?"

"No, because Araujo is taking this thing very seriously, and God help anybody who doesn't take him seriously. So far I haven't even earned bed and board. Which reminds me. When we gather for dinner will everyone be there?"

"Except Kalos."

"That figures. Anyhow, when you arrange the seatings for dinner—"

"Maggie does that."

"Whoever. Just make sure I'm next to Belle Rountree. For business reasons." I stood up and pointed at the blank screen. "And since this seems to be where we came in—"

Pablo was as good as his word. My two shirts handed over to his custody were neatly hung away in my closet ready for wear. I put one on, adorned myself with a necktie, fitted myself into the more subdued of my jackets, and made my way to the dining room well ahead of the eight o'clock dinner hour. If I was to be planted next to Belle Rountree, now was the time to make sure of it.

Maggie was alone in the dining room dealing out place cards. The table, not quite the length of a bowling alley, was already set. That is, half of it was set—one service at the head, five on either side. The rest of it, highly polished and naked, just glimmered off into the distance.

I gave the lady a warm hello; she gave me a distinctly cool hello. With a choice of asking why the coolness or checking out the cards, I checked out the cards. Quist was to be at the head of the table. To his right, in order, were to be Sharon, Calderon, Maggie herself, Scott Rountree, and Araujo. To Quist's left would be Holly Lee, Kightlinger, Lou Hoffman, Belle Rountree, and Milano.

Mute Maggie suddenly found her tongue. "When you were having your little dialogue with Sharon, did you say something about me?"

"No. Why?"

"Because she just acted pretty damn strange. She came into my room and said to put you next to Belle at dinner. Then—no warmup, just a quick pitch—she said she had asked you to take her with you to New York when you left, and you had told her you wouldn't."

"Oh, Jesus," I said, "the confidentiality kids," and Maggie retorted, "Never mind that. You know Sharon and I don't have any secrets between us. What concerns me is what came next. She said, 'Of course, if you were the one, he'd jump at the chance, wouldn't he?' And then just walked out and left icicles forming on the ceiling."

"She did ask me if I liked you. I answered truthfully that I liked you. That is as far as it went."

"I'm not so sure, Milano. I realize it should be an ego trip for any woman to have Sharon Bauer regard her as a rival, but it does my position here no good at all. If for your own devious reasons you did suggest to her—"

"I didn't. Anyhow, isn't a foundation grant coming along in a month or so to take you to Europe for a long stretch? That makes your position here very temporary, I'd say."

"It'll be even more temporary if Sharon decides I'm an undesirable element. And that grant money isn't in my hands yet."

"A big healthy grant, I trust."

"Big enough. Fifty thousand."

"I'm afraid I couldn't match that. Still, if you do get it, and on your way to Europe find you can spend time in New York—or even postpone Europe awhile—"

"No."

"I'll settle right now for a maybe."

Maggie said angrily, "You are so goddamn obvious, Milano. No matter how you really feel about Sharon, you're going to punish her every possible chance, aren't you? All right, that's your business. But don't try to set me up as make-believe competition just to help along in the project."

I said amicably, "Whatever you want," and when she said with distrust, "That's it?" I said, "Sure. I take it Daskalos doesn't play hermit out there in his cottage. He does show up at the barracks here now and then."

"Now and then. He visits Sharon when he's in the mood. And he uses the library."

I asked, "Is there a phone in that cottage? I didn't see any number listed for one."

"His request. But he does have a phone there. And, yes, he uses it quite a bit. Incoming calls from the Coast mostly. Believers who have a problem they want him to help with."

"But he does make calls himself when he's in the mood."

"Yes. Now, if you'd kindly explain why you're so—"

"Company's coming," I warned. Because, in fact, company, led by Quist in his wheelchair, was on its way through the door.

Caviar and champagne may have been laid on for the Christmastime guests here, but what Araujo's temporary staff came up with for dinner was a sort of Cuban festival of foods, featuring a rice, black bean, and meat stew, backed up by pitchers of watery sangría. The service was uncertain, confused, and sometimes downright dangerous. None of this did anything to relieve the atmosphere around the table, which was considerably thicker than the gravy that came with the stew.

Quist, taking this in with a mordant eye from his wheelchair at the head of the table, now and then stirred up general conversation which at best was fitful. At one point he did it at my expense, reminding me that I owed him a dollar for my defeat in the water Olympics in the morning. After I had passed the bill along the table to him he lectured in high good humor about a legendary Australian swimmer, Murray Rose, whose kickless style had inspired him to his own present necessary technique. And winning ways.

Belle Rountree, up to then silent as she cautiously picked her way through her viands, searching out proteins from carbohydrates, leaned toward me. "One dollar is cheap. He took Scottie for a hundred at chess. Up to then Scottie thought he was a chess player."

I laughed politely. "Any other ways he hustles his guests?"

"Bridge. There could be a table set up after supper. He and Maggie Riley against all comers. Beware."

"She play a good game?"

"Fair. But he's master level, I'd say. Squeezes blood

104

out of a hand. And talking about blood, how are you making out pinning the tail on the donkey?"

"So-so."

"But you think it is somebody right here at this table?"

"Could be."

"Could be. You're a regular little chatterbox, aren't you?" She looked at me inquiringly. "Or is it possible you've got me down on your list and find the subject a mite uncomfortable?"

I said, "Your name's down there all right. And, no, I don't find the subject uncomfortable at all."

Belle carefully laid her fork on her plate. Kightlinger, further down our side of the table, and Calderon, directly across from him, were warming up to an argument about cinematography. Something about West Coast cameramen not knowing how to handle the South Florida sunlight. Kightlinger said they didn't, Calderon said they did, their voices rising with each exchange.

Belle suddenly said to me, "What the hell makes you think there's even a remote chance I'm the one?"

"Motive. And opportunity."

"What motive?"

I said, "You don't like what's happening to your husband's movie script. That script is being butchered by Daskalos' orders. Maybe more than that, you don't like what's happening to your husband. He seems to be buying Daskalos' bill of goods. Falling under the influence."

"And that's your dimwitted idea of a motive?"

"It is. How much of a motive I don't know, because I don't know you that well. Or your husband. However, I take it you're proud of his work. He's no hack. Right?"

"You couldn't be righter. He's dealt with very respectfully in literary circles. Real literary circles. And a hack doesn't take years of sweat to write a novel. In thirteen years he's written five of them, working full time."

"And a movie script."

"He put everything into it, just the way he does with his novels. He couldn't be a hack if he tried."

"And that's how you want it?"

"That is damn well how I want it. When *The New York Review of Books* defines him as an authentic talent and gives him two full pages—"

I cut in, "All the same, when Daskalos said to either cut the heart out of that script or no movie deal, your husband went right along with it. Isn't that what they call hacking it out?"

"No," Belle said in a light voice. "Pride."

"Pride?"

Belle said, "Five books. Great reviews, damn few sales. I'm the breadwinner of the family. Scottie brings home a small piece of cake now and then. That's not easy for him to live with. If this picture is made, it means he'll put real money in the bank for the first time in his life."

"I thought he was already paid for the job."

"Option money. Ten percent. The other ninety comes when principal photography commences."

"But the way things are you'd rather not have it commence."

"That is—was—one beautiful script before it went on the operating table. And I know, because my job is evaluating literary properties. I work for Wyeth and Wyeth. Ever hear of them?"

"No."

"Literary agents. Old-line. Still think quality writing is the name of the game, not packaging. It was Scottie's luck that they're the ones he mailed his first manuscript to. And I was the one who picked it out of the slush pile. Want the rest? He came to New York from Des Moines with a cardboard suitcase and a portable typewriter, and I worked with him on the book until it was ready for the publishers, and eventually we got married. And, as you can see, we're still married. End of story."

Lou Hoffman, on Belle's other side, had been drawn into the argument about cameramen. He was plaintively explaining that, as director, he had already contacted Pruitt on the Coast, and Pruitt didn't need lessons in handling any sunlight. After all, he had been on the

106

camera for Mike's last picture, which was shot in Texas. What about the sunlight there?

Kightlinger said, "Oh, for chrissake," and reached for the pitcher of sangría. The too-helpful waiter behind him grabbed for it simultaneously, and wine spilled on the table. The look Araujo gave his hired hand was a dotted line with daggers on it.

Belle said to me, "Anyhow, if you think everything was hunky-dory with this picture until Kalos showed up, you're way off. I'll grant Sid Kightlinger one thing, he started off with good intentions. But he didn't have the guts to follow through."

"Meaning?"

"Meaning that as soon as he was told he might get backing if he signed on Mike Calderon, he jumped at the chance. He knew Mike is all wrong for the part—he's at least ten years too old for it—and he also knew that Mike grabs control of any picture he's in. Which is how Lou got picked as director, which is how Holly Lee got picked for a lead. And she is worse than all wrong."

"And Mrs. Quist?"

Belle said grimly, "Sheer denial on Sid's part. There's a couple of bedroom scenes in the script. Very essential, very explicit." She motioned with her chin toward the head of the table, where Quist was being entertained by the cameraman argument. "Our Mr. Quist made it plain from the start he intends to be right there on the set any time his wife is in action. I ask you to consider the consequences."

I considered them. "Interesting," I admitted. "Do you think Daskalos might have put Quist up to playing chaperon?"

"Kalos? He wouldn't have to. Why?"

"Because at breakfast you suggested I check out why Calderon was so hot to play in this picture, and why he'd like to see Daskalos dead. The hot part, according to my sources, is that Calderon has a dire need to crawl into bed with Mrs. Quist without her husband or a cameraman present. Is that right?"

"Dire is the word for it."

I said, "And since Daskalos stands against such immorality—"

"That's about the size of it. You don't know Mike. He is not one to live with frustration. And if scaring off Daskalos—"

I cut in: "You didn't say anything at breakfast about scaring him off. You said you believed a murder impended."

Belle looked unhappy. "Well, if you'd gotten an eyeful of that poor mutt laying there. And that blood—"

I said, "Murder was the word you used. And Calderon was the one you pointed at."

"All right, then I withdraw the nomination. I never meant Mike was a killer. A general all-around son of a bitch, yes. Not a killer."

"Are you sure of that?"

Belle said in exasperation, "Ah, come on, Sam Spade."

"Do you know anything about Calderon's marriage? His family?"

"Know what? He's got a wife and kid somewhere. You want to see pictures of the kid, ask him. He carries a string of them around."

"And that's all you know about him?"

"If I knew more, I'd be happy to run a seminar on it for you!"

Her timing was bad. Kightlinger, loudly upholding his end of the argument about cameramen, caught Quist watching him with amusement and stopped short in midsentence. Belle's words came out clearly audible in the sudden silence. Every head turned toward us.

Belle said brightly to the company, "I was responding to a third degree by Mr. Milano. He's been making like a detective."

"That's what he's here for," said Quist just as brightly.

There was bridge after dinner in a sort of game room furnished with a few card tables, a bar, big-game trophies, mostly carnivorous, and a lineup of Pachinko pinball machines. Cigars and brandy were offered as a preliminary. The cigar Araujo lit for me was good. The brandy I sampled wasn't in the class of Quist's private stock.

Hoffman and Kightlinger lingered briefly over drinks, then departed to look over the day's work on the script, Holly Lee trailing after them. Quist and Maggie made a bridge partnership against the Rountrees. Sharon and Calderon paired off in armchairs which Calderon had dragged into knee-to-knee position. At the bridge table Belle Rountree said, "Tenth of a cent a point is still my speed," and Rountree grumbled something at her.

There was a bowl of brass slugs on a table near the Pachinko machines. Araujo watched me drop a slug into a machine and test the plunger. He said in an undertone, "Do me a favor. Instruct me to place a man on twenty-four-hour duty at the front door here."

I glanced at him and saw he wasn't joking. I said, "Sure. You do that." I released a ball and it tinkled musically against nailheads. "Now tell me why I'm doing you this favor."

"Because Mrs. Quist hates to have security people placed where she can see them. They make her nervous. It's why she can't stand the apartment in town: the security is very conspicuous there. But since she has such faith in your judgment about these things—"

"Isn't it up to Mr. Quist?"

"Not when she gets emotional about it."

"I see. So if she does get emotional this time, you lay the problem on me."

Araujo said, "You do agree that a man should be on duty at that door, don't you?"

"I do. All the time. And wide awake."

He went off to attend to this. I played a couple of games, scoring badly. Then I moved over to the bridge table and took up a position at Belle's shoulder. She hadn't underestimated Quist's skill, but he had easy pickings here. Belle herself handled her cards competently, but Rountree was one of those pugnacious types who had to take the bid and play the hand no matter what. That was fatal against a team like Quist and Maggie who would guilefully ease him into overbidding, then double him and set the hand, piling up the points. Each time this happened he would blast his wife for her bidding, and Belle took this graciously, nodding her head in acknowledgment of the sins she hadn't committed.

Her husband's style of play gave her plenty of chance to be dummy hand, and she finally seized one such opportunity—after laying out the hand and getting the predictable calling down—to rise from the table and move a safe distance from it. *En passant* she said to me, "Got a cigarette you can spare?"

I followed her across the room and lit the cigarette for her. She sat on the arm of a couch, puffing away. Finally she said, "You never do see Scottie at his best, do you?"

"In my line of work you don't often see people at their best."

"I know. Like a gynecologist." She waved aside smoke. "Is he on your list of suspects, too?"

"Yes."

"So he thought. And it's one of the things upsetting him. You must know the idea is ridiculous."

I said, "If he's not our joker, he doesn't have anything to worry about."

Belle crushed out the cigarette in an ashtray. "You really ought to come up with some shiny new clichés.

And, for that matter, a plausible suspect. Otherwise, somebody here is having a good silent laugh at you right now."

"Maybe not. After all, nobody's been eliminated from the list yet."

Belle said sweetly, "Not even Holly Lee?"

"No."

"You have to be kidding. That baby bitch rates as one of the prophet's truly dedicated ass-kissers."

I said, "She's an actress. A pro. Do people like that stop acting when they're offscreen? Can they?"

Belle said, "Well, I might debate that under other conditions. Right now I'm all for it. Stick it to her, Sam."

She rose to go back to the table. I blocked her way and said, "This morning you described the notes to Daskalos as Biblical. Is that because you recognized some Biblical lines in them?"

"Do you remember every little thing you hear, Sam?"

"I remember that because a line in the first note's been bothering me. It sounds familiar but I can't place it. 'I am in Hell.' Is that from the Bible?"

Belle said, "Not that I know of. It's just that the tone of those things is Biblical. Grim prophecy. Jeremiah on the loose. Damn scary too. At least for a civilian like me."

"You're a judge of writing. Would you say they're well written?"

"Very well written in their gruesome, simplistic way. Almost as if—" She stopped short there, and when I encouragingly said, "Yes?" she said, "Go do your own homework. I've got a cold deck of cards to warm up."

The game ended after two rubbers, the Quist-Maggie team splitting eight dollars in winnings. Good nights were said, Sharon switching on all the sapphire power in those eyes as she said it to me. Maggie lingered to turn out lights, and I lingered with her. Throughout the game she had managed to suggest that I wasn't visible to her. Now, her finger on the light button, she had to take notice of me. "After you, Mr. Milano."

I said, "You know, there's something really funny

111

about all this. About us. You've cooked up a juicy scenario where I'm Sharon's betrayed and vengeful lover. You don't like me in that role, which is understandable. At the same time, you won't let me explain that I'm being wildly miscast."

"I don't see why my opinions should matter to you, Mr. Milano."

"But they do, Miss Riley. Now, may I revise that scenario?"

"If you'll kindly—"

"Just listen. For one thing, I have no intention of taking Quist's money and getting into bed with his wife simultaneously. I admit that three years ago it would have been different. But contrary to what you said earlier this evening, three years can be a very long time. And a very instructive time."

Maggie took her hand away from the light button. "I've known Sharon almost that long. It seems to me she's very much the same now as she was then."

"Or even more so. That's the point. That time in England I had the idea that I was easing her out of her dreamland into good healthy reality. But last night while she and I were talking I realized that far from moving closer to my reality she had hauled me right into her dreamland. Sir Galahad come to rescue a soul-stirring, pill-popping princess from all the dragons besetting her."

Maggie said, "I seem to remember that the Sir Galahad analogy was mine."

"It was. And somehow it helped reinforce my impression that Mrs. Quist is a lot tougher than she looks. She is not really the plaything of fate. She knows what she wants when she wants it, and she has an uncanny way of getting it. An amoeba type. Sort of flows around the desired object and ingests it."

"In fact," Maggie said tartly, "quite the beautiful monster."

"Nope. Just a beautiful mixed-up kid. But put all that aside, Miss Riley. Fix your eyes on the bottom line. Which is that when I indicate to you my pleasure in your company it is not because I'm trying to play

112

you off against Sharon, God forbid. And with that settled—"

"I'm not so sure it is, Milano." But her mood was plainly changing from dark to light.

I said, "Try me out. I have a fireplace and the makings. We can stroll upstairs—"

"No." She glanced at her watch. "What we can do is sit down in my office and discuss my book. Remember my Van Gogh book? We were supposed to get to it sometime today. There isn't much of the day left.

"Your office?"

"Uh-huh. My plain old office. No fireplace, no fixings, no bed. Did you read that Jack the Ripper study I gave you?"

"I dipped into it. If you're wondering whether I found any connection between him and Van Gogh, no, I didn't. But right now—"

"Right now, Milano," said Maggie, "let's go to the office and sign in."

On the way to the office I saw that there was now a uniformed security man stationed inside the building's front door, a Pablo type but even more youthful. He gave us a chipper, two-fingered salute as we passed, and I returned it. Out of his range, I said to Maggie, "Araujo told me Sharon's got a thing about bodyguards clustering around. That it's why she'd rather stay here than in the duplex in town. Is that true?"

"Yes. I can't really blame her for it. Andrew never lets her go out of the apartment in town without someone tagging after her with a gun under his armpit. It can make for a pretty claustrophobic lifestyle. Here at least she's got space to ramble around in by herself."

I said, "Is it possible—just barely possible—that it isn't only kidnapers Andrew's concerned about? That he's found himself a neat device this way for keeping tabs on his wife every minute of her time?"

"Anything's possible," Maggie said shortly.

"Now, that's what I call a clear-cut equivocal answer." I took notice that this time instead of pushing open the office door she had to unlock it.

She waved me to an armchair and sat down sideways at her desk to face me. A cold wind rattled the doors opening on the terrace and filtered through the room. I said, "Considering the money Quist put into this place, why not central heating for times like this?"

"It's only a cold wave. It never lasts long."

"That's what the Chamber of Commerce would like me to believe. All right, I'll warm up hearing about Van Gogh. Start with those overheated days in sunny Arles."

"No." She was very serious. "I'd rather start by asking you what your image of him is. Not as a painter. As a man."

"My image of him? Oh, I suppose a martyr to his art. At least as neurotic as Sharon Bauer."

"That all?"

"I really didn't study for this test. Well, let's say his heart was in the right place. He sympathized with the poor and downtrodden, used them as subjects in his early stuff. Financially dependent all his working life on his kindly brother, what's-his-name."

"Theo."

"Theo. Near the end, while he was in Arles, he went from neurotic to psychotic. He threw a series of fits. There was that business of his cutting off an ear and presenting it to some surprised hooker. Finally he killed himself. I'll settle for a gentleman's C."

"You don't rate it," Maggie said without humor. "He was not psychotic, the way you mean it." She motioned at the bookshelves. "His collected letters are there, including the ones from Arles. If you want to see a demonstration of coherence and brilliance, read them."

"When I have time. Now, would you mind telling me how Jack the Ripper fits into this? That's the part I'm here for, isn't it?"

"I'll get to that. First let's fill in some of the record. Vincent was not only sensitive to the downtrodden, he agonized over the condition of the downtrodden female. Notably those broken-down streetwalkers who serviced him now and then. He was eccentric and awkward, so women of his own class shied away from him. So he did turn to prostitutes. And felt intense guilt because of this. Not on moral grounds, but from an understanding of the degradation they suffered in their lives."

I said, "I've known a few hookers who would not quite—" and Maggie cut in sharply: "You wouldn't have known the kind he did. Not the diseased, used-up kind you could buy with a crust of bread. Like the one he took to live with him out of pity. In his Amsterdam period. A woman named Sien. The pathetic, miserable, ugly bottom of the barrel. And pregnant into the bargain. He didn't have much more than a crust of bread

115

himself, but he made a home for her and her children for almost two years. When Theo suggested that this didn't make sense, especially since the woman was ungrateful and abusive, Vincent simply answered that it was his duty."

I said, "I'm beginning to see a remote Jack the Ripper connection. The Ripper butchered prostitutes, Van Gogh salvaged them. Beyond that, you've still got me wondering."

"But you must know that the Ripper didn't just butcher them. He mutilated them. And in one case he cut out the victim's kidney and mailed it to the police." She leaned forward, her eyes bright with intensity. "Don't you find that enlightening, Milano? That particular act? In terms of Vincent's self-mutilation?"

I mentally shuffled these pieces together and finally came up with the required enlightenment. "Are you telling me that Van Gogh cut off his ear and gave it to a prostitute to compensate for what Jack the Ripper did to another prostitute? Is that your theory?"

"It's more than a theory, Milano. And once and for all it wipes out that whole patronizing image of the mad artist committing a random self-destructive act. What Jack the Ripper did in mailing the police that bloody remnant of his victim was the last straw for Vincent, the ultimate obscenity. What Vincent did in response was to perform an act of atonement. Because slashing off his ear and giving it to a prostitute was exactly that."

I said, "Hold it. You're summing up for the jury, not offering evidence."

Maggie drew a deep breath. "All right, the evidence. Start with the fact that the six murders definitely attributed to the Ripper took place between early August and late November of 1888. The newspapers first broke the story in September."

"The British papers, that is."

"Naturally it was the London papers first. But papers everywhere—including France—picked it up very quickly. I've got a whole carton of clippings from

French provincial papers in the Midi. Which Vincent must have read."

"Or which you assume he read. When exactly did he do that ear job on himself?"

"December twenty-third, that same year. The woman he gave it to was simply known as Rachel. Evidently a favorite of his in what was called Brothel Number One in Arles. Paul Gauguin was sharing life with Vincent then. He frequented the same place."

I started to say we could leave out Paul Gauguin and such, but Maggie said urgently, "No, we can't. Now listen. He and Vincent had a ferocious quarrel that day. They were always at each other's throats, but this time it seemed to have been worse than usual. It was right after the quarrel, when he was alone, that Vincent slashed off part of his ear and took it to Rachel. The Ripper case was now a topic of conversation everywhere. Consider that these two men—Vincent suffering torment for the victims, Gauguin born to abuse women—would have been diametrically opposed on that topic. Consider that to end any such argument Gauguin might very well have said: 'Well, what the hell can you do about it anyhow?' And when he was alone Vincent in a frenzy of shame and despair saw what he could do about it. And did it. And has been misunderstood for it ever since."

She waited, looking as if she were ready to land one on me if I said the wrong thing. I took my time trying to come up with the right one. "At the very least I don't think I'll be able to look at a Van Gogh again without allowing for this."

"How generous of you."

I said, "Don't be unfair. You've worked out a theory, and taking everything into account—especially the timing of events—it does make some sense. After all, a foundation's willing to put money into it. But you must know yourself it needs substantiation." I pointed at the bookshelves. "For instance, in those van Gogh letters is there any mention of Jack the Ripper?"

"No. But there are other materials to be searched

out. Letters, journals, diaries hidden away and forgotten by people he came into contact with during that period."

"Like Gauguin?"

"Not Gauguin. I'm positive that whatever he and Vincent said to each other on that subject went to the grave with him."

I said, "That's quite a handicap to start with, isn't it?" and Maggie shook her head vigorously. "Just the opposite. The quarrel they had that day has never been cleared up. And Gauguin was far from reticent about his quarrels. Why would he keep the nature of this one secret unless he felt deeply guilty about it? Unless something he said during it drove Vincent to self-mutilation and giving the ear to Rachel. Of course it would have been said in sarcasm—'If you're so damn sorry about a piece of meat being cut out of a dead whore, why not just square accounts for her?'—something like that. But Vincent would have seized on it literally."

"I'll concede the possibility. But those other materials you want to search out—do you really expect to come up with something worthwhile?"

"Of course I do. I'm not starting out cold on this. I already have leads in Provence and Amsterdam to go on. And that's where I'd like your professional advice."

"About what?"

"I have to locate about a dozen people in Europe. I don't have addresses for most of them, just identification. But these are the people who could give me further leads to where private material's been stored away. Now, how would you handle all that?"

"Through a Paris agency I know."

"A detective agency?"

"That's right. I can give you an introduction to the head man there. But you have to keep one thing in mind. It's expensive."

"How expensive? After all, if I get that grant, I'll have fifty thousand dollars to work with."

I did some quick calculation. "One man, full time, will cost you half of that in a year. Allowing for some

118

polite padding of the swindle sheet. Which you have to allow for."

Maggie said, "So in two years—" and suddenly the room was pitch-dark. The chandelier and the desk lamp might have been blown out by one of those gusts banging against the doors. I was in a tunnel, no light at either end.

"Oh, hell," said Maggie. "A blackout. It's all right. There's an emergency generator. It'll come right on."

It didn't.

Objects in the room started to take on vague form. I used my lighter to read my watch. Eleven-ten. I asked, "Do you have a flashlight handy?" and Maggie said, "Right here." A drawer scraped open. A flashlight beam stabbed across the room and imprinted a full moon on the far wall.

I took the flashlight, handed Maggie the lighter. I said, "I'm going out. Meanwhile, do what I tell you, no questions. Phone Daskalos. If he answers, just tell him power'll be on soon and that's all. Then phone Calderon, do the same thing. If either of them doesn't answer, keep calling him. If and when you finally get an answer, note the time. What's your watch say right now?"

It agreed with mine. Maggie said, "But Kalos is probably asleep already. And most likely Mike's in Miami Beach."

"Never mind that. Just start working the phone."

I left by way of the terrace, a handy shortcut, and the gas lamps along the way made it an easy run to the service building. I wasn't the first on the scene. Right outside the generator room, among a concentration of flashlight beams, there was a huddle of figures, Araujo prominent among them. He was in an undershirt, his belt hung unbuckled. He looked furious. A uniformed man sat on the floor hunched forward, his teeth clenched, his eyes closed. Blood was smeared on the man's scalp.

I said to Araujo, "What about Daskalos?" and he answered, "Everything's all right there." He motioned at the dazed man on the floor and spat out, "Stupid as a rabbit. He heard a noise, he walked out here to see what it was, and somebody gave it to him right on the head."

I said, "Before or after the blackout?" and Araujo said impatiently, "Just before it, naturally. And this is not a power failure." He pointed through the heavy wire mesh of the closed cage gate at the jacks in the panel, both now at the horizontal. "See that? The outside feed-in and the emergency generator—the two of them pulled. And whoever did it got away with this idiot's key, too. I had to send to the office for mine. And his gun was taken. That's a lovely thing to have on the loose around here right now."

I said without too much hope, "You realize an assault like this is a police job, don't you?"

"No. The boss would raise hell about it, and for good reason. It isn't worth it."

"How about a doctor? That looks like a hard wallop."

Araujo said contemptuously, "Not enough to dent a head made of concrete. A couple of aspirins, and he'll be fit as an ox. Until I have a little talk with him."

A man came running in with the key. Araujo opened the gate of the cage, shoved the jacks upright, and lights came on. He picked up the phone on the desk to show me the severed cord. "Didn't miss a trick." There was a porno magazine open on the desk, one corner of it weighted down by an empty beer bottle. Araujo flung the magazine through the open gate at the injured man, missing him by inches. He yelled at the man, 'Sitting here jerking off, is that it? On overtime pay?"

He fired a volley of Spanish at the others, then took my arm and led me outside the building. Considering his barrel shape and stumpy legs, he could move fast. He said, "I'll get a cart and give you a lift back. Then I want to check out the cottages."

"Good idea. Mind if I join the party?"

"Not at all. But"—his voice became warmly ingratiating—"there's something else that must be done right now. Something I'd like you to take care of."

"Yes?"

"Explain to the boss what just happened. Very diplomatically." He managed a laugh. "Tomorrow, he'll have cooled off a little, you know? But right now—"

I said I had no objection to being the bearer of ill tidings, but that our first stop should be the main gate. Araujo raised his eyebrows at this. "Anyone who tried that way out would be marked. The security there is very tight."

"That's what I'm counting on."

He trotted upstairs to his office and came down in shirt and jacket. Then, plainly irritated by this detour, he steered us in the cart to the main gate. "A waste of time," he muttered, pulling up at the gatehouse.

His mood changed as he questioned the man on duty. Yes, said the man, someone had driven out not long ago. During the blackout. Mr. Calderon. Absolutely. No question. Mr. Calderon.

Araujo wheeled the cart in an arc and headed toward the main building. Fifty yards down the driveway he brought us to a jolting halt. "Jesus," he said in bewilderment. "Michael Calderon. But a man like that? Why? For what reason?"

I said, "I can give you a good one, but it has to be kept strictly between us. If you object—"

"No, no. Not at all."

I described Calderon's marital mix-up much as Shirley Glass had passed it along to me long distance, and Araujo nodded grimly. He said, "I'll tell you this much. If I were deprived of my child—my only son—by such means—"

"I know. But that doesn't guarantee Calderon's our man."

"Oh, sure," Araujo said going along with the joke.

"I'm serious. Calderon takes off for town every night. I wanted to check out the gate now to see if he did it tonight. And he did, knowing he'd be identified. If he did pull off the blackout, it means he was unbelievably careless about getting away with it."

"So he was."

"But," I said, "up to now our jokester's been anything but careless about his operation. Those two pieces don't fit together."

Araujo said incredulously, "You think this puts him in the clear?"

"Not at all. I think we don't jump to any conclusions someone might want us to jump to. We just keep going as we are. Wherever that is."

Araujo kicked the cart into motion. "Fine," he said. "You just tell me when we get there."

Maggie, still at the phone, had company. Quist, wearing a robe and with a towel arranged like a turban on his head, sat in his wheelchair, his face gray and drawn with pain. He said to me in a hoarse whisper, "That was no accidental blackout, was it?"

I said, "One second," and looked inquiringly at Maggie. She put down the phone and said, "All I get from Kalos is a busy signal. Mike's phone rings, but he doesn't answer. Mr. Quist had me call Security a few minutes ago. The man there said Kalos was all right, and that you and Virgilio had gone somewhere together."

I said, "Araujo's checking out the cottages now. Calderon's taken himself a drive into town. For the time being, everything's under control."

Sharon walked in just in time to catch this. She had changed from dinner gown to tee-shirt and shorts, and there was transparently nothing under the tee-shirt. She took Quist's hand and said to him, "You see? Now you can come inside and take your sleeping pills, can't you?" Without giving him a chance to answer, she explained to me: "He was in the Jacuzzi when the power went off. And stayed off. And Maggie's phone was all tied up. I had an awful time getting someone to help."

Quist said to her, "Please, dear"—he took a couple of deep breaths as if he had to pump up his lungs to get them working properly—"everything is not under control." He glared at me. "All right, what the hell happened?"

I described what had happened, omitting further mention of Calderon. Quist wasn't buying that package.

"You said our Mr. Calderon's taken himself a drive into town. When did he leave? Precisely when?"

"A few minutes before the power was cut off."

Quist leaned back in his chair. "Now, isn't that interesting?"

"It is. But I'll put it to you the way I put it to Mr. Araujo. If Calderon is the one, would he aim a finger straight at himself? Mr. Araujo seems to think he would. I have my doubts."

Quist took his time evaluating this. He finally said, "Virgilio's specialty is security, not your kind of work. So in this situation I'll go along with you. Up to a point. Now, what about Mr. Daskalos, who doesn't answer the phone. Is he still in your sights?"

Before I could respond, Sharon protested: "But if Kalos is in meditation—" and Quist said in the voice of a kindly father to an idiot child, "He may not be, dear. Not necessarily." He painfully shifted his legs. Then he focused on me again. "Well, what about Daskalos?"

"If he's the one, I can't understand why. That doesn't stop me from wondering about it."

"And where does that leave us? Any comments? Any advice?"

"One comment. From the evidence tonight, our perpetrator can now be rated dangerous. One piece of advice. The same advice. Pack everybody out of here."

Quist looked at Sharon. Her lips compressed tightly and her face went stony. He gave her an almost imperceptible nod. Maggie, taking this in, seemed troubled. "Really, Andrew, it might be wise—" and he snapped at her, "Wait!" He thrust out that Roman senatorial jaw at me. "Tell me this, John. And no hedging. Do you think there's any danger to Mrs. Quist if she remains here?"

"Well, when you have someone with a loaded gun—"

"God damn it, I asked a straightforward question. Do you believe in your professional capacity that this someone with a loaded gun represents a threat to Mrs. Quist? Yes or no?"

"If you put it that way, no."

"All right. In that case, try to comprehend that this is

our home, my wife's and mine. And no one—no one on earth, Mr. Milano—is going to drive us out of it because he's in a mood to do mischief. If I had my legs, no one would dare attempt that mischief. Well, this old cripple still has his moral legs. And a large helping of old-fashioned self-respect." He had to fight for breath to wind up the lecture. "However you're going about your job, Mr. Milano, bear that in mind."

He released his hand from Sharon's, spun the chair around, and took off in high gear. Sharon hesitated, then went to the desk, leaned over it and spoke to Maggie in an undertone. She departed, carefully not looking in my direction. I said to Maggie, "What was that about?"

"She asked me to give you a couple of letters I've been keeping locked up for her. They're in my bedroom. Wait a minute."

The letters were in their envelopes, which were still tucked into the larger Watrous Associates envelopes I had used in returning them. I thrust them into my jacket pocket and asked, "Do you know what's in them?"

Maggie shrugged. "She wanted me to read them but I wouldn't. But I think I have an idea what's in them."

"So do I. You know, she really shouldn't be laying all of this on you. Dividing your loyalties between her and Quist."

"I manage to live with it." She looked at me curiously. "You realize you could have wound up the party right now, didn't you? Just by telling Andrew she was in danger. For whatever reason."

"No, he's too smart to fall for whatever reason. He'd want a good logical reason, and I couldn't offer any. If I tried to fake one, I'd be standing here right now mopping egg off my face."

"Uh-uh." She shook her head. "Not you. Never."

"If that's a compliment, thanks. But I suspect it isn't. What's on your mind, Maggie Riley?"

"A large question mark. You know Sharon's just about given up on Kalos, don't you?"

"Yes."

"And you know that even if someone bombed this

building, she'd want to keep the party going. Because if everyone was cleared out of here, you'd be on your way back to New York."

I said, "There we enter the realm of speculation. I'm going back Thursday anyhow. I don't think one day—"

"She does. She's fighting for time to turn your no into a yes, and one day can make the difference. After all, as you pointed out, she does seem to have a way of getting what she wants."

"Usually. But where does the question mark come in?"

"Right where you could have told Andrew she was in danger, and didn't. If you had—and despite Andrew's brave oratory—this place would have been emptied in one hour flat. So that question, Mr. Milano, is: Are you now on your way to changing that no into a yes? Because if you are, I'm the one who'll be left here to deal with Andrew in his loss. And I'd like to get my foxhole dug before the event."

"Then put away your shovel, Private Riley. You won't need it."

Maggie looked doubtful. "You mean that?"

"I do. And as a favor, you might try to convince Sharon of it."

"Oh, no, Milano. Not me."

"All right, then do me a different favor. This Milano thing you're addicted to. On first introduction I told you it was Johnny to my friends. Such as they are."

Maggie said in a flat voice, "Sorry. That's Sharon's word. I'd just as soon not infringe."

"Which is really a crock. I mean, this business of always putting Sharon between us. On second thought, is it Sharon? Or is it the shade of somebody named Donnie Maxwell? The guy who used to share your living arrangements. And worked on your book with you."

Maggie said accusingly, "She told you about him."

"Yes. With great admiration."

"And that's where we drop that subject, Milano. Right here."

I said, "Look, there comes a time—" and the phone rang. I cursed Alexander Graham Bell and all his works as Maggie answered: "No. I don't have to. He's with me here." She handed it to me. "It's Virgilio. Sounds like more trouble."

Araujo said to me, "I'm at Cottage B. Next-door to Mr. Daskalos. I had to use this phone."

"Something's happened to him?"

"No, no. But there is a problem. Yours really. I'll have a cart pick you up right away. I'll be outside Mr. Daskalos' place."

"I won't need a cart. I'll be there in a few minutes."

I put down the phone. Maggie looked sick. "My God," she said. "Kalos."

"Easy does it, baby. He's all right."

"You're not just saying that?"

"Take my word for it," I said, "he'll live to worship at least one more sunrise."

I made it to the cottage in a series of wind sprints, and Araujo was waiting for me on the terrace. He motioned toward the door. "I explained to him about the blackout, the assault. And what happened? He acted as if I had come to rape him up his asshole. I had no right to interfere with God's ways, he said. All very well, I told him, but there is the matter of his safety. Was I wrong in telling him that?"

"No. Then what?"

"He said his safety wasn't my business. That what must happen will happen. Then he handed me this."

Araujo thrust the sheet of paper at me. The same heavy bond. The familiar typeface. But this time a message boiled down to the absolute minimum.

Wednesday, January 25
Tonight!

I looked at my watch. "We're ten minutes into Wednesday. When did he get this?"

"He won't say. He sits there. He won't say anything now."

"Did he have any visitors today? Your man next-door keeps track of that, doesn't he?"

"Until the blackout, no visitors."

"During the blackout?"

Araujo lowered his head to his chest as he weighed this, making four chins out of two. "No. For someone to have been in the service building pulling those switches, and at the same time to be here delivering this—"

"All right, who brings Daskalos' meals to him here?"

"You know him. Pablo."

"Well, is there any chance at all that Pablo—?" and Araujo shook his head with granite assurance. "None. Pablo is my nephew. A little free in his ways, but a good boy. Not one to play dangerous tricks on his Uncle Virgilio."

I held up the paper. "So assuming that no one delivered this today and that it didn't fly here by itself—"

"I know, I know. Shit." Araujo spat in a high arc over the flowering hedge fencing in the terrace. "So we have the possibility that Mr. Daskalos writes these notes to himself. And we have the possibility that Mr. Calderon caused the blackout. Talk about pieces of a puzzle not fitting together, how about those two?"

"Maybe Daskalos can help with the carpentry." I put a hand on the doorknob. "Is it open?"

"Always. He insists on that."

The door led directly into a living room which was much more Holiday Inn than the Plaza. There was a low fire in the fireplace, a straightback chair facing it. Daskalos in sweater and slacks sat at attention in the chair, hands on knees, eyes fixed on the layer of glowing coals behind the fire screen.

I asked Araujo: "Where's the phone here?" and Daskalos, without turning his head, said, "I did not give you the freedom of this house, John Milano."

"In that case I'll have to borrow it." I looked at Araujo, who seemed acutely uncomfortable with this byplay. "Well?"

He waved. "There's a phone in the bedroom. An extension in the kitchen."

"One of them's off the hook. Let's go see."

The bedroom phone was in order, the kitchen phone was dangling from its wall box. I replaced it and asked Araujo for Miss Riley's number. She answered immediately, apparently expecting the worst. I soothingly told her that all was well, slid around the question of what Araujo wanted me for, and asked her to leave a wake-up call for me in the morning. Or, better yet, how about doing the waking up herself. But not for sunrise Adoration. About, say, eight-thirty.

She said, "Sorry. I'll be leaving for the museum then. I have a nine-o'clock appointment there with Andrew's lawyer."

"Then how about my going along? It may be my only chance to see the collection." I allowed her a long silence, then said, "And I have a question to ask about your book. That should be the place to ask it."

"Well"—she still wasn't ecstatic about the idea—"all right. I'll have someone bring you a breakfast tray at eight."

I hung up the phone. Talking about trays, there was one full of dirty dishes on the work table below the phone. Also a bowl of fruit, another of salad ingredients, and a couple of large bottles of oil and vinegar. Evidence that even messiahs facing the moment of reincarnation can have lusty appetites. Araujo helped himself to some grapes, popping them into his mouth as I looked around. When I pushed open the outside door I saw that the back of the building was only a few yards from the edge of the bluff overlooking the beach. I could make out steps set into the sandy slope and lines of whiteness in the distance—waves breaking on the shore—and very little more than that.

We went back to the living room. I stood between Daskalos and the fireplace, forcing him to contemplate the neat crease in my J. Press slacks. Araujo respectfully hovered at a distance.

I said to Daskalos, "In my church, suicide is a mortal sin. Any opinions on that?"

No answer.

I said, "You'll observe I'm sticking to theology, teacher. No zodiac, no Tarot, just high-minded theology. Or is it too high-minded for you?"

This brought him out of his catatonic state. "Self-destruction is a sin, John Milano. Only God can give life. Only God may end it."

"So if one connives at his own death, teacher, isn't he guilty of that sin?"

Daskalos raised his face to mine, indications on it of

131

a malignant temper heating up. "You are like the serpent, John Milano. A corrupter. But the woman you tried to corrupt resisted you because of the strength I gave her. That is why you challenge me now, isn't it? Because when you would have barred her way to The Path—"

Araujo was taking this in with open-mouthed fascination. I said sharply, "Oh, knock it off, Daskalos," cutting him down in midflight. I gave Araujo a hand signal. "Let's go. We're wasting time here."

On the terrace, he said to me, "What was he talking about? You looked ready to go for his throat."

"Hardly. And he was only talking the same nonsense he handed me this morning. In the morning I'm fresh, I can take it. But I am definitely not in the mood for that kind of crap at this late hour."

"Yes. Of course. But you're supposed to keep him under close surveillance tomorrow night. Tonight, that is. To be with him right here. The way he talked, I don't see how—"

"We'll worry about it when the time comes." I said.

It was Holly Lee who, in pajamas primly buttoned up to the neckline, answered my knock at the door of Cottage C.

She was alone, she said. After spending time in Sid's apartment watching Lou and Sid work on the script she had walked back here and gone straight to bed. As far as she knew, they were still at the script.

In the living room, she sprawled in an armchair, legs stretched out exposing long, bony feet. On the sole of one foot was a tarry-looking oval, the size of a quarter. On the heel was an identical discoloration. Araujo, I took note, seemed much interested in these stigmata as I brought Holly Lee up to date on events. Between the fitful yawns of one just awakened she expressed polite surprise at news of any blackout and polite concern about the assault on the security man. Neither the yawns, the surprise nor the concern seemed altogether convincing.

Araujo did considerable throat clearing, then said to her: "So you slept through the blackout."

"Mmm. It would be easy to sleep through, wouldn't it?"

"Of course. But at any time since you got back here were you outside on the beach?"

She turned wide, innocent eyes on him. "There's not much to see out there this time of night, is there?"

"No. That's true." He gave me a look which indicated that he was itching to get something off his chest.

He finally had a chance to do it outside. "She was lying. She was on the beach only a little while ago."

"What makes you so sure?"

133

"Those stains on her foot. There was an oil spill from some boat yesterday, and there are drops of it all along the sand. Walk there in the dark, and you'll sure as hell come up with spots like that. No question she was lying."

I said, "She'd have had time enough to make it to Daskalos and back without trouble either. But what about your man in the boathouse? Wouldn't there be a risk of being seen by him?"

"In this darkness? Almost none." He said something in firecracker Spanish, then shook his head ruefully. "In translation that means I should have taken early retirement. What a night. First Mr. Calderon, then Mr. Daskalos, now her. And what comes next?"

"Mr. and Mrs. Rountree," I said.

But only Mrs. Rountree was at home. After the bridge game, Belle said, she had come back to the cottage while Scottie had joined Sid and Lou at their labors on the script. Early in the blackout she had tried to get Riley on the phone, but that line was always busy. So she had called Sid's apartment and spoken to her husband. They were sitting it out, he had told her. She supposed they were now back at work. "And what the hell was going on? Blackouts in New York were a way of life, but down here—"

I cut into this: "When you phoned your husband who answered?"

"He did."

"He took a call on Kightlinger's phone?"

Belle said testily, "If Sid and Lou were sitting over the script, why not?"

"You said you called during the blackout. You mean they were sitting over the script in the dark?"

For a moment she was off balance. She quickly righted herself. "Well, he could have been the one near the phone. What's up, Sam? There's more here than meets the eye, isn't there?"

"Yes. That blackout was pulled off deliberately. And somebody coldcocked a guard to get at those switches."

"My God." She seemed to be trying on different expressions. "And you don't know who it is?"

"No."

"Well, obviously it wasn't me. And if Scottie and Sid and Lou were keeping each other company . . ." This trailed off. Her eyes narrowed. "That look on your finely etched features, Sam. You're not thinking, are you, that I'm just handing around cheap alibis?"

"Are you?"

"No, I am not. But remember what I told you about somebody having a good silent laugh at the way you're playing gadfly with the wrong horses? Take it from me, he's having that laugh right now."

This, I learned as I fitted myself into the golf cart, was what stuck in Araujo's throat. He said, "Somebody laughing at us. And she's a clever woman. For all we know, she's the one."

"Not acting alone. She'd have to be tied in with someone."

"Her husband, naturally. Consider the way she gave him his alibi. Do you believe she really spoke to him during the blackout?"

I said, "Whether she did or not, odds are she's on the phone with him right now bringing him up to date. So if she was lying, he'll be all ready to back up the lie. Anyhow, I'll stop off at Kightlinger's rooms and see what goes on there."

"Without apologies," said Araujo. "I have to tip my hat to them. You don't." He started the cart rolling bumpily over the flagstones. "I've had a bellyful of this business. Now with a loaded gun around, God knows where. And this last note to Mr. Daskalos. Why the hell did he give it to me if he didn't want anything done about it?"

"That's a good question. Are you going to see Quist in the morning?"

"Yes."

I handed over the note. "Then give him that for his collection. I'm going to the museum with Miss Riley after breakfast. I'll see you when I get back."

"Did you have a chance to tell the boss about the blackout before I called you?"

"I did."

"How did he take it? No"—Araujo made a gesture of dismissal—"never mind. I can imagine."

"Whatever you imagine," I said, "should just about cover it."

Interestingly, the security man was no longer at the door when I walked into the main building. I waited for his return a fair time before giving up on it.

Kightlinger's sitting room was a fog of tobacco smoke. Kightlinger and Lou Hoffman were at a coffee table littered with papers. Rountree was in an armchair working hard on a pipe. None of them seemed surprised to see me walk in without invitation. All plainly had their armor buckled on and shields in position.

It was Kightlinger who told me that, yes, Belle had just phoned with word of my visit and the story of the blackout and assault. Terrible. Jesus. This was past being any kind of joke. He spoke. The other two fixed me with fishy eyes and now and then, as if synchronized, nodded agreement.

I let their spokesman talk himself out. Then I asked him, "Were all of you here during the whole thing? Nobody left at any time?"

Kightlinger said unctuously, "Well, you know Scottie didn't get here until after his bridge game."

"I know."

"And since he did, nobody left here. Not for a minute."

"A minute wouldn't mean much," I pointed out. "Twenty minutes would be closer to it."

"Forget it. Nobody left to go make blackouts or give any poor slob his lumps. But one thing we did, Milano, besides sit here and sweat out a tough writing job. We did some thinking about who the mystery man could be. Want to know who we picked?"

"Can't hurt," I said. "Might help."

137

"All right, then you take a good look at Daskalos himself."

I looked, instead, at Rountree, allegedly one of the messiah's admirers. Pipe clenched in his bulldog jaw, he remained fishy-eyed and imperturbable. I said to Kightlinger, "Why Daskalos?"

He seemed offended. "Does that surprise you?"

"No. But if you can come up with a convincing reason for his killing a dog and splitting a man's skull, I might be surprised."

"All right," said Kightlinger, "he hears voices. God is telling him to do it."

The cadaverous Hoffman waggled a forefinger at me. "There's nothing to smile about, Milano. I was involved with Daskalos for a while. Take it from me he's authentic. Not rational by materialist standards maybe, but authentic. He believes in what he preaches."

I said, "In that case, why his concentration on show business people? Why doesn't he just carve himself a begging bowl and go out into the world with his message?"

"Because it isn't that kind of world anymore. Want to score with a heavy message today? Lay it on people with a heavy image."

"Which," I said, "suggests that he's right down there with all those nasty materialists, doesn't it?"

Rountree picked up the ball. "That's not quite as clever as it sounds, Milano. Cheap cynicism rarely is."

I said, "I'll keep that in mind," and took the three of them in, one by one. "Now, what you folks have to keep in mind is that if Mr. Daskalos is our poltergeist, he couldn't have stirred up all this commotion by himself. So there must be somebody lending him a hand. Any idea who that is?"

One by one, each of them gave me a shake of the head.

"Well," I said, "the room number is twenty-eight. When your team hits on an answer just pick up the phone and pass it along."

I offered them a genial good night in departing. I didn't get any in return, genial or otherwise.

I removed Sharon's letters from my jacket, hung up the jacket, kicked off my shoes, and stretched out on the bed to do my reading there. I knew at once that this was no way to do it. It had been an eighteen-hour day, and every one of those hours had a grip on my eyelids and was dragging them down. Close them, and that would be it until the wake-up call.

My body protesting this cruel treatment, I hauled it off the bed and across the room to the dresser, where reposed the balloon glass with its still-ample supply of Quist's private stock. Airing fine cognac, I found, in no way diminished its impact, at least not if you took a proper dose. Standing there, I opened the Watrous Associates' envelope postmarked July—easily done, because it was already unsealed—and opened the envelope within it, which was barely sealed with a lick.

Instantly, a familiar, tantalizing, traumatic scent rose to my nostrils.

Fleurs de Rocaille.

I didn't remember the letter being scented this way when it was delivered to me by Shirley Glass in my office, but I could have been wrong about that. If I weren't—if it had been doctored for maximum effect— that was indeed dirty pool. The dirtiest. Because the effect now may not have been maximum, but it was certainly undeniable.

Six sheets of embossed paper, both sides of each sheet covered with a childish scrawl. *Johnny dear*, it started, and then in page after page of rambling prose it set forth the case for our reunion. *Do you remember what it was like that time?* popped up frequently. That time when we walked to the village . . . That time when we talked about . . . That time when we put the mattress in front of the fire and we . . .

I did remember. I also remembered what she could have only seen in a rearview mirror: gravel from under her Jaguar's tires stinging my rainsoaked, uncomprehending face.

At one point, midway in all that scramble of reminiscence and explanation of her present woeful plight, she came perilously close to undoing a lot of the damage that gravel had done. Close to poetry, in fact. *You made me feel real, Johnny. I never felt real before. I don't now. But you made me feel real.*

My grip on the situation was suddenly becoming slippery. I reinforced it with a huge belt of cognac. And by hard contemplation of my correspondent's dazzling ego.

Apparently, it had never entered her mind that Johnny might now himself be committed to some other female of his choice. Not much of a tribute to me in that. Much less, in truth, than that paid me by Maggie Riley in her wary circling away from me.

Anyhow, since Mrs. Quist and I had pretty well hashed over the subject of the letter during the past day and a half, there were no real surprises in its first ten pages. Then came page eleven.

She wanted to have a baby. Not Andrew's baby, because that would only make everything worse than it already was. My baby.

I startled myself by saying out loud in exasperation, "Oh, for chrissake, Sharon!"

My baby. Why fight it?

She would come to New York and move in and we would have a baby. Sundays, if I weren't out negotiating with fences like my friend Hennig, we would take turns pushing it around Central Park. Of course, once a week she'd phone Andrew to make sure he was getting his rest and not overdoing the Jacuzzi.

As she had put it in that earlier passage, she didn't feel real. I was beginning to feel unreal myself.

The other letter, dated December, at least had one foot on the ground. A mere four pages long, it opened with a restrained blast at me for having returned the previous message unread. Then came The Plan. She was at the bottom, I was the only one who could help her, and she had to see me right away. Christmas week there would be a big party on the estate, a lot of people would be around all week, and if I just showed up as her guest, we'd be able to get together in private now and then. With all those people around. So please don't write or call or anything, just come. And when I get to the gate just ask for her.

Signed, in case I didn't get the nature of the invitation, *Your Sharon*.

Well, smarter people have made dumber plans. I could have been introduced for what I was, an old acquaintance who had once helped solve a professional problem for her. In that mob of yuletide freeloaders—eighty of them, Araujo had said—I could have maintained a low profile. On the estate, there would have been no hired guards hovering over the lady's shoulder, one point of contention with her husband where she had been winner. As for the promised privacy, there might have been a French farce quality about the hunt for it, but you can't have everything, can you?

I burned both letters in the fireplace, reduced them to powdered ash, and floated into bed on a tide of cognac.

And dreamed a whole series of dreams which all started at different points and all wound up at the same one. Maggie Riley was watermelon-bellied pregnant with my child and was sore as hell about it.

In the bright light of morning, however, when I met Maggie in front of the building where her car would be delivered, she turned out to be—allowing for a subtle and pleasing female roundness of belly just below the waistband of her slacks—gratifyingly flat where it counted. And in a mood for talk. She had just sat in on the briefing session where Araujo described to Quist what had gone on during cottage inspection. What happened after I left Araujo? Did I get to see Sid and Scottie and Lou?

I said I had.

"And?"

"And they all fingered Daskalos."

"They did?" Maggie said. "You know, Virgilio's beginning to wonder about it himself. About whether Kalos hasn't somehow rigged up all this and gotten the others to go along with it. Wild as that sounds."

"Wild events make for wild theories. Could Araujo offer a reason for any such rig-up?"

"No, but there's this new message Kalos seems to have pulled out of his hat." She frowned. "About that message. Do you think it was written the same time as the others?"

"Probably."

"I'm glad to hear that. Anyhow, there's the way Kalos came up with that message. And there's Holly Lee's visiting him during the blackout—"

"There's no hard evidence she did."

"Virgilio thinks she did. You don't?"

I shrugged. "Listening to Wynken, Blynken, and Kightlinger, I got the impression that while they were all pointing at Daskalos what they really had on their minds was Calderon."

"Mike?"

"Mike. He's got good reason for wanting to lay out Daskalos. And he was flagrantly close to the scene of the crime last night. If he turns out to be the bad guy, Kightlinger sees his movie package go up in smoke. So he lines everybody up to make a case against Daskalos."

Maggie made no comment on this as the car was brought up and she got behind the wheel. We were down the road some distance before she broke her silence. "Virgilio said you had a bad time with Kalos yourself while you were at it. What was that about?"

"Oh, that. The messiah started to open up about me and Sharon, and there was Araujo listening with his ears fanned out. No sweat. I managed to shut up Daskalos before any damage was done."

"You're sure?"

"Yes. Anyhow, if I'm asked what woman I was trying to lure from the path of righteousness, I'll just say it was you."

"Thanks a lot. But what about the blackout? Why would anybody want to pull it off? Whoever it was."

"Using cop's logic, whoever it was wanted to get hold of a loaded gun. Of course, logic could be the most misleading thing to use in this case."

"That's a big help," said Maggie.

The mansion housing the Quist Collection was not as big as I had anticipated but big enough, a three-story stucco roofed with Spanish tile. Inside, the guards on view were obviously first-string men, rugged, trimly uniformed, and capable looking. Quist's tax lawyer was waiting there in the anteroom. Maggie introduced me as a friend of the family, and then departed with him up a flight of stairs, leaving me to do my own exploration of the collection.

As it turned out, I had plenty of time to do it in, from Courbet to Gauguin. It was a collection frozen in time, the second half of the nineteenth century, about three dozen oils and two Degas ballerina bronzes, but it was superb in every way, not a clinker there. And, of course, there was the pleasure of discovering master-works I'd never seen before even in reproduction. Maggie's pets, for instance, the two Van Goghs. One was a self-portrait which must have been painted not long after the ear-slicing episode, the scarf which served as bandage concealing the severed ear, the eyes looking calmly into the observer's. For all anyone knew, the subject could be thinking of the way he had atoned for the sins of Jack the Ripper.

I made the rounds of the main gallery a few times before I tried the door at its far end and found myself in a small reading room. Shelves of leatherbound books, and on the one exposed wall a picture that had nothing to do with any other here: a John Singer Sargent por-trait, life-sized, of a handsome young woman in shirt-waist and floor-length skirt. I already guessed before I looked at the inscription on the brass plate that this had something to do with family, and so it proved. Mary Henrietta Lucas Quist. Quist's mother, probably.

When Maggie finally showed up she confirmed that Mary Henrietta was indeed Quist's revered mother and a lot of old-time Boston money, but she was plainly not interested in anything by slickster Sargent. So it was back to her Vincent and a lecture on him which, when my feet started to ache, I broke into by asking her how her business with the lawyer had gone.

She shook her head. "Not good. He had a list a mile long of the requirements we'd have to fulfill to get tax exemption. Including opening the doors to the public on a limited basis."

"And Quist won't go for that?"

"Not at all. Nohow. Now and then a certified scholar, okay. Not the public and buttered popcorn."

I said sympathetically, "And here you are, right in the middle of the brouhaha."

"Nice word," Maggie said. "You don't hear it often in these parts. But I'm completely with Andrew in this. Going public means going into show business. A new loan exhibition to set up every month. Finger-painting lessons for the kiddies. Lectures with slides for people who don't give a damn about art but want to talk about it at cocktail parties. That's what a curator's come to mean nowadays. It is not my line of country."

"Maybe not. But you sure can deliver a powerful lecture when so moved."

Her face reddened. "Well, I'm not lumping you with the general public. You're here, aren't you? Come to think of it, you said one reason you wanted to come along was to ask me a question about my book. What question?"

I thought fast. "What led you to a Van Gogh–Jack the Ripper connection? Where did it start?"

She looked reproachful. "You're faking it, Milano. That is strictly a nothing question."

"Caught in the act. But now that it did come up I'm curious about the answer. What is it?"

"A Woman's Lib get-together. About seven or eight years ago. They had a speaker—well, I'll admit she was a little far out—on the inherent sadism of the male when dealing with the female. She used the Ripper murders as the classic example. When she mentioned the dates it suddenly struck me how they fit Vincent's crisis. That was it."

I said, "Out of compost do marvelous flowers spring."

"Very poetic. Sticking to prose, how about recommending an agency in Paris that'll do my investigating for me and won't break the bank?"

"How about an early lunch somewhere around here? If I make the recommendations then, it's a business lunch. Tax deductible."

"No."

"Quist told you to cooperate with me, didn't he?"

"Yes, but he didn't—"

"Never mind the fancy footwork. Just cooperate. You pick the place."

Which turned out to be a Kentucky Fried Chicken emporium.

With separate checks, of course.

At the garage, Maggie took the golf cart shuttle to the main building, and I took a walk upstairs to Security headquarters. Araujo, hollow-eyed and in a bilious mood, was alone there, consoling himself with a foot-long sandwich and a bottle of beer. I reported on my interview with Kightlinger and company; Araujo, through hunks of sandwich, described the search for the missing gun. The service building and garage area had already been combed. There was now a platoon beating the bushes along all pathways. Oh yes, and when Mr. Calderon had come driving in at dawn he had—not very graciously—submitted his person as well as his car to a thorough search. So far, no gun.

I said that this was no surprise. What was surprising was the way our movie people were now lining up against Daskalos. Indeed, the chief of Security himself had mentioned to Miss Riley his growing suspicions of the gent. How about that?

Araujo said irritably, "I know. You were the first one to come up with the idea. Well, now it really begins to make sense." He leaned far back to empty the beer bottle down his throat, then thumped it down on the desk. "What the hell, look at the way they alibi each other. The way they have us running around in circles. Playing games with us. And Daskalos has to be the one pulling those strings."

It was now Daskalos, I observed, not Mr. Daskalos. An official demotion.

I said, "It seems to me that some of those strings would pull right back."

"So what?" Araujo leaned forward, elbows on the

desk, hands spread wide. "Look, I'll tell you my position. Everything is happening by schedule, whoever arranged that schedule. And for whatever crazy reason. So by midnight it should be all over, because that's how the schedule reads. Then tomorrow the sun comes up, and everybody pretends none of this ever happened. A big joke. Right?"

"A pretty bad joke."

"Very bad. Now, the job is not to let it get worse. Pin everybody down tonight; make sure they stay pinned down."

"How?"

Araujo said with satisfaction, "My idea, and the boss went along with it. He'll be showing one of Mrs. Quist's movies after dinner. That takes us right past the deadline. And everyone will be sitting there except Daskalos."

"And Calderon."

"He'll be there. The boss already had it out with him. With all of them. Drinks and toilet privileges provided. Meanwhile you'll keep Daskalos close company. One problem with that, of course. He won't like it."

"Possibly not."

"Then what if I joined you? It might help cool the temperature."

I shook my head. "You shouldn't be pinned down there."

"I can easily—"

"No. I'll handle Daskalos; you keep an eye on the others. Which reminds me. Your man at the entrance to the main building wasn't around when I got back there last night. What happened to him?"

Araujo grunted with what might have been weary resignation. "During the blackout, Mrs. Quist got him in to help the boss out of the Jacuzzi. When that was settled she just told him to clear out of the building. No more job at the door there."

"And Quist let her get away with it?"

"I told you how she was about that kind of thing. Visible security. But the boss was only being diplomatic. This morning he let me know in private that

147

when the movie is on I'm to have a man right there at that door. Diplomacy, you know?" Araujo grinned broadly. "When I was a kid there was a very big calypso song. Big even in the Havana joints. 'Always marry a woman uglier than you.' Good advice, hey? Especially if you don't want to spend all your time being diplomatic with your woman."

"Very good advice. Did you follow it yourself?"

He laughed. "Hell, no. What man does?"

Not Andrew Quist. That was for sure.

When I came into the main building company was straggling down the hallway from the dining room. Calderon, decked out for tennis, a couple of rackets under his arm, the other arm around Holly Lee's waist—evidently, if Sharon's wasn't handy, any available female waist would do—and behind him Kightlinger and Lou Hoffman in close conversation, with Belle Rountree and her Scottie bringing up the rear.

As the procession filed out the door, Belle pivoted and headed back in my direction. "I want to talk to you, Sam."

"Sure. My apartment is your apartment."

"No, it's just for a minute." She had put on her make-up carelessly; its line of demarcation was clearly visible along her jaw. She looked me over. "So it seems the prophet finally met his match."

"Daskalos?"

"Uh-huh. Seems like he got on his high horse with you last night, and you belted him right off it."

"Where'd you pick that up?"

"Oh, from King Andrew himself. When he was laying down the ground rules for tonight's fun and games. You do know he's leaning toward the idea that the prophet is our guilty party, don't you? Which, it so happens, is the direction the rest of us now lean."

"Including your husband? And Holly Lee?"

"Scottie, despite a bent for the mystical, does have his logical side. Holly Lee is wavering. It all adds up to a very big score for you, Sam. Andrew let it be known that from the time you showed up here you had the prophet dead in your sights."

149

I shook my head. "The most dangerous mistake right now—" and Belle flashed out, "Oh, stop playing it so goddam cagey. Kalos is the one, and you know it. In fact, you personally know that son of a bitch a lot better than you've been letting on."

"You're way ahead of me, Mrs. Rountree."

"Am I? Than shift into high and catch up. Daskalos isn't any stranger to you. Because three years ago you handled a very hush-hush case for Sharon Bauer and you must have run into him then. And sized him up for what he was. That's why, as soon as you walked in here you had his number. So all this private-eye performance you're putting on is just going through the motions, isn't it?"

"Some of it," I said. "Not much."

She was momentarily at a loss for words. Then she said, "Honest John Milano himself. All right, how about an honest answer to this one?" Her voice hardened. "Are you covering up for Daskalos? The Sharon Bauer effect maybe? She's sold on him, and you don't want to bring tears to those pretty eyes?"

"Mrs. Quist and I—"

"Oh, don't give me that Mrs. Quist shit. Sid Kightlinger said that before she hooked Quist she had a name for humping everything in sight. And there you were, personally hauling her out of God knows what kind of mess. Are you saying she missed a mouthwatering dish like you on the way around?"

"I appreciate the compliment. I don't think Mrs. Quist would."

"That's no answer."

I said, "Then how about trying the question on Mike Calderon? He was more than available to the lady when they were making their picture together. Weren't you the one who told me it didn't do him any good at all?"

"Because he probably turned her stomach. I know he turns mine. So that's still no answer."

I said, "Look. What you want me to do is pin the rap on Daskalos. Then the movie-making proceeds without his spell being cast on it. Right?"

"With an extra little touch, Sam. From what I heard,

last night you almost laid him away yourself. That gives me the feeling that you hate his guts as much as I do. So why not tell Quist to dump him right this minute? Why wait? Nothing's going to happen tonight while you're with him. Nothing can."

"And tomorrow he'd only be dug in here deeper than ever."

Belle said with satisfaction, "Now you're zeroed in, Sam."

"Just in time to zero out, Mrs. Rountree."

Always leave them laughing. Or, at least, with their mouths hanging open.

In my bedroom, I headed straight for the cognac on the dresser but was pulled up short by a note on the desk. An awkward penciled scrawl: *Mr. Milano, please call Miss Glass N.Y.*

I called, and when Shirley answered I said, "This is John Milano, Miss Glass," the formality being the Watrous Associates' method of warning that there might be other ears tuned in.

Shirley said, "I wanted to check on when you'll be back, Mr. Milano. There's those Monday appointments I put over. Should I definitely set them up for tomorrow afternoon?"

"Yes."

"I'll see you then, Mr. Milano. Oh, by the way"—she was burlesquing secretarial dignity—"your sister sent us another I.D.C. this morning. For the usual three-hundred-dollar fee. And Mr. Watrous was very nice about it. Had no objection at all to our handling it."

"Thank him for me," I said. "But not passionately."

I put down the phone, went over to the dresser, and finished the cognac, chugalug. Then I hefted the empty balloon glass and measured the distance to the far wall. I caught myself in time. From the feel of it, look of it, and sound of it when I pinged it with a fingernail it was Baccarat.

Instead, after brief reflection and with the cognac taking hold nicely, I gathered together the glass, the book on Jack the Ripper, and Quist's senatorial terry-cloth robe and carted the load down to Maggie's office.

She was typing away busily but stopped to take account of me and my cargo. "You didn't have to bother with that, Milano. One of the help would have taken care of it."

"No bother." I deposited the glass and robe on a table, then put the book back in its place on the shelves. The shelf below, the travel book section, had gaps in it. I asked, "What happened to that new book about Bligh and the *Bounty*?"

Maggie's fingers were poised over the typewriter. "If it isn't there, Andrew may have it. He's napping now, but later on—"

"No." I made myself comfortable in the chair across the desk. "I could probably write that book myself. First grownup book I ever read that turned me on was the old Nordhoff and Hall *Mutiny on the Bounty*. After that, I read everything I could about Bligh and his merry men. Won an essay prize at New Utrecht High putting it all together."

"Bully for you. Now, if you don't mind—"

I said, "Saw both pictures half a dozen times each. The Gable one and the Brando one. Want to know something?"

"No."

"Well, the Brando one got panned, but it was a bum rap. It was a lot more authentic than the Gable one."

Maggie removed her hands from the typewriter. "Milano can't you see I'm trying to work?"

"All right," I said, "no more conversation. I'll just sit and yearn for you in dead silence."

"No, you will not." She squinted at me. "Are you stoned?"

"Not too much. Just enough to make me feel at ease in company."

"I thought you looked fuzzy around the edges. Well, stoned or otherwise, you're not making me feel at ease." She sounded really angry about it. "So just go away. Right now."

She went back to her typing with a will, I went to the door with regrets. The typing suddenly stopped. "Wait a second, Milano. About dinner tonight. Do you want to be next to Belle again?"

"Under no conditions."

"Oh? The romance over already?"

"Far from it," I said. "I just want to wind it down before it gets out of hand. I have other fish to fry. Other Kentucky chickens, too." But, lips set, she was already banging away at the typewriter again.

To eliminate those fuzzy edges I took a cold shower—one loud yell and the worst of it was over. Then, Japanese style, I ran a tub hot enough to steam up all the glass in the bathroom. For want of reading matter I settled on the automobile map of the Miami area provided by the house and was admiring the unlikely names of some of its communities—Opa-locka especially—when I became aware that I was not alone.

I lowered the map, and there in that steamy atmosphere, like Venus risen on the half shell, was Mrs. Quist.

And in no mood for preliminary sparring. "Did you read my letters, Johnny?"

I said, "Jesus, didn't it strike you that if you could come waltzing in here like this, somebody else could?"

"I locked the outside door. Did you read them, Johnny? Especially that first one?"

"Yes." If she was going to be removed, it would have to be with a firm hand prodding her on. I got out of the tub and went to work on myself with a towel. "We'll talk about it later, Sharon."

"No. And you're not really worried about someone walking in. Only about the way things are between us. You know what I said in that letter makes sense, and you don't want to admit it."

"About my being elected to father your child? Sharon, it doesn't make sense. It just makes bad comedy."

I went into the bedroom and started dressing. She followed and sat down, hands clasped in her lap. Im-

154

movable. She said, "You don't know anything about biology, do you?"

"Biology?"

"I'm twenty-six. Pretty soon it'll be too late for me to have a baby. And I want one. But it can't be by Andrew. It has to be by someone I want to share it with. I'm not asking you to get married, am I?"

Sufficiently clad, I went into the sitting room and unlocked the hallway door. Sharon came right along. Again she perched herself on a chair, hands clasped in lap. Still immovable.

I said, "Look, let me spell out our relationship in very simple language. I am handling a case for your husband. That is our relationship."

Her eyes got very shiny. "I don't believe it." Her voice, even more husky than usual, now had that box-office little croak in it. "I know you hated me when I freaked out in England. But now that you understand about it, you don't any more. You're just afraid it might happen that way again. It won't, Johnny."

"It won't get a chance to. But forget England. Just get it into your head how I feel about being maneuvered down here so cleverly. About being put into this screwball situation. About Araujo being told to keep his security people far away from you, so that you can work out your future with me in private. And what about your guru? You're ready to kiss him off, but not as long as he's an excuse to keep me here. Hell, I told Maggie you weren't manipulative, but now—"

I put on the brakes too late. Sharon said stormily, "You talked to her about me?"

"No more than you talked to her about me."

"It's not the same! She doesn't feel the way I do about you!"

"For chrissake, cool it," I said, "or they'll hear you down in Key West. I'm here on a job. Anything I talked to Maggie about had to do with that job."

"Including me? Is that why you took off with her this morning? So you could take her to some motel to ask if I was the one who killed that dog? And hit that man over the head?"

I said wearily, "You know better than that."

"I'll tell you what I know. That I didn't maneuver you down here. That Andrew and Virgilio kept talking about somebody who could investigate what was going on here and still keep his mouth shut, and I finally mentioned you, that's all. And I don't want any guards standing around watching me, because I've had enough of everybody watching every move I make." She laid the edge of her hand across her throat. "I've had it right up to here, do you understand? And I'll tell Kalos I can't be a Believer any more when it's time. And it is not time while somebody is trying to kill him."

I said soothingly, "Yes, of course. It makes sense that way. It really does."

She looked doubtful. "Do you mean that?"

"Yes. It's just that this place is a pressure cooker right now. We're all emotionally shooting from the hip. But talking things over rationally, some other place, some other time—"

"Tomorrow. In New York."

I had to draw the line somewhere. "No, that's irrational." Those eyes signaled stormy weather again. I said, "Be fair, Sharon. You've never asked me about any personal commitment I might have in New York, and you should have. Because there it is, and it can't be untied on one day's notice. Or," I added pointedly, "on ten minutes' notice, the way it's done in merry old England sometimes."

She looked shamefaced. "You don't know how many times I thought about that day, Johnny. But no more. Please don't ever talk about it any more."

"It's a deal. Your part of it is not to say anything or do anything that could make things difficult for me right now. I've got this weirdo case here, I do have that commitment in New York—"

"Only in New York? You're sure there's nothing going on here with one of the natives?"

"Nothing. So help me." I took her hand and eased her up from the chair, carefully avoiding body contact. I steered her to the door. "Remember," I advised her, "it's not how fast you travel, it's only the direction you travel that counts."

She gave me a smile. "Now you sound like Kalos, Johnny. I'll see you at dinner."

Ten minutes later the phone rang. Maggie. She said coldly, "Thanks a lot, Milano."

I didn't have to ask the question. I asked it anyhow. "What's that mean?"

"It means I was just put in my place by someone who dropped in on her way home from the detective works. From now on, Milano, whenever you see me coming give me all the room you can spare. You can count on my returning the favor."

"Ah, come on," I coaxed, but I was coaxing a dead line.

There was a barely visible moon showing when I went down to the oceanfront to catch Daskalos' sunset performance. A sparse audience this time: Holly Lee, Lou Hoffman, Scott Rountree. Nor did they join the messiah on the beach, but huddled together at the head of the stairway, watching from there.

Despite this poor box office, Daskalos, the old pro, put his heart into his work. Clad in the same minimal costume, he faced us—and the flaming horizon to the west—and went into the bonecracking simulated crucifixion, closing with thanks to the sun for having done a good job this day. The moon was clear, the stars bright by the time he wound up the act.

The audience did not disperse, however. It huddled even closer together and engaged in some muttered talk while Daskalos stood watching from the tideline. Suddenly, Holly Lee moved down the stairway. Hoffman was after her at once, grabbing her arm and pulling her to a standstill. Rountree promptly followed, and there was another low-voiced conference. During it, the two men took turns glancing my way. Either my presence, even at a distance, disturbed them or I was an item on their agenda. Meanwhile, Daskalos waited.

He could have saved himself the wait. The conferees—Hoffman still with that grip on Holly Lee's arm—finally walked up the stairs and headed toward their cottages.

Daskalos went his way.

I went mine, back to Apartment 28, to do some meditating of my own before dinner.

Meditation, however fruitless, makes time fly. The fruitful part came when I joined the dinner party a few minutes late to find that Maggie, in rearranging her seating plan, had delivered Holly Lee right into my clutches. ESP maybe? I hadn't asked for it, but here it was. Belle Rountree was now Quist's lefthand partner at the head of the table; Holly Lee, in Belle's former seat, was planted between Lou Hoffman and me.

Cool to me at the outset, presenting her animated side to Hoffman, she warmed up a little when I commented on the food we were being offered. No Cuban special this time, it was French cookery of fair quality. Holly Lee nodded wisely and leaned toward me. "Catered," she said in an undertone.

"That explains it."

"You can thank Mike. He got so pissed off at the meals this new bunch of help is cooking up that he laid it right on Andrew. So they had some restaurant in town do all this and ship it in."

"Mike speaks his mind," I remarked, and with all the sweet gravity of Alice in Wonderland, Holly Lee said, "Why the fuck not?"

He was speaking his mind again, loud enough to be heard the length of the table. Now it was on the comparative merits of California and Florida, with an acid-tongued Quist making it a sort of cudgel versus rapier duel. Sid Kightlinger, nervously watching his superstar and his moneyman have at it, several times tried to point out that each side had merit, and each time was batted down by both. Lou Hoffman, apart from those occasions when Holly Lee addressed him, looked abstracted. Scott Rountree stolidly tucked away everything that was put before him. Belle, never saying a word, went through that familiar business of extracting noncarbohydrates from her plate and then masticating them with distaste. Sharon, right in the combat zone between her husband and Calderon, seemed beatifically unaware of both. Maggie seemed as unaware, but not beatifically. Head down, shoulders hunched, she sat there as if posing for a statue of dejection. Araujo, eating hugely, drinking lustily, slowed down as he took notice of this stricken image beside him. He gave her a fatherly pat on the shoulder, nudging her into an interest in the goodies before her. She thanked him by wrenching away the shoulder.

Holly Lee must have been digesting the tail end of our conversation along with her hors d'oeuvres. She leaned toward me again. "You don't have something special going about Mike, do you? Like thinking he's the one wrote those notes and all?"

"No. Nothing special."

Holly Lee nodded. "That's what the word is. I mean, like you figure Kalos is it. Right?"

"Except for the teaser. Why would he be going through all this to wind up dead?"

"Oh, that. But he doesn't really die. He comes back."

"In another form?"

"Well, in another body, if that's what you mean. But Believers will know him."

I said, "Even so, doesn't it bother you to think of his getting killed? The violence, the pain, all that part of it?"

Holly Lee's face clouded. "Well, sort of."

"Is that what you were talking about with Lou and Scottie right after services?"

"Not exactly." She hesitated, then came out with it. "Look, if Kalos is the one doing all this stuff here, then there's really nobody else out to kill him, is there?"

"Isn't there?"

Holly Lee said heatedly, "What's the big question? Nobody else would be out to kill him. But then—well, he'd have to kill himself, wouldn't he? And he's supposed to be against that kind of thing. So that's what I wanted to ask him about. And that's what Lou and Scottie don't want me to do."

"Why not?"

"They said I shouldn't get in the way. That if Kalos is, like, you know, God on earth, then everything that happens is his plan. And a Believer shouldn't go around asking questions about it."

I said, "But Lou and Scottie aren't Believers. Where do they come to hold your proxy?"

"What?"

"Why take their advice about it? Do you think they have a real concern for Daskalos?"

Holly Lee slowly shook her head. "I think they just want to see what'll happen, that's all. Especially Scottie. All writers are flaky that way. He and Lou already talked about maybe there's a story in all this. So that—"

I cut in: "Aside from that angle, why buy their advice?"

"Mister, I've got a part coming up in their picture. A big one. Oscar Supporting Actress big. But so far, nobody's handed me any contract to sign."

"I see."

"That makes you a very smart detective. Anyhow, you'll be with Kalos tonight, won't you? So whatever happens, you'll be on top of it."

I said, "Right on top of it," and was going to add the assurance that nothing would happen, when Hoffman, plainly troubled by this dialogue outside his hearing range, reclaimed his starlet. And made sure to keep her reclaimed, leaving me to extract what entertainment I could from the table talk.

It was during my filet of sole that I saw Araujo suddenly swivel his head toward the hallway door. When I looked the door was already closing behind whoever had signaled a presence there. Araujo got to his feet, motioned me to follow suit. In the hallway outside was Pablo.

"Any luck?" Araujo asked him, and when Pablo shook his head Araujo said venomously, "Goddam

161

gun." He turned to me. "This was a good opportunity for it, so I just had him check out those cottages for that lousy gun. Mr. Rountree's and Mr. Hoffman's." He regarded Pablo with a flinty eye. "You didn't disturb anything there, did you?"

"No chance."

"I hope not," Araujo snapped. "All right, back on the job," and Pablo, accurately gauging his uncle's mood, moved off on winged feet.

I said to Araujo, "Two cottages out of three. Not bad. But not perfect."

"I realize that. But when you're with Daskalos maybe you can do something about that. Handle with care, but"—he made a circling motion with his hand—"look around, you know? There's not many places there you can hide a gun."

"He and I will be coming to a fast understanding," I said. "That'll be part of it."

"It would help. One other thing. I want to check out those two apartments upstairs. Fifteen minutes should do it. Meanwhile, you'll have to keep an eye on Mr. Calderon and Mr. Kightlinger. If either of them shows any signs of leaving the table to go upstairs, stall them. It would be one fat embarrassment if I got caught digging through those dresser drawers."

"I'll do what I can. Does Quist know about this search without warrant?"

Araujo winked broadly. "He'd be shocked at the idea. But what was that with Miss Otis at the table? Did you get anything new from her about last night?"

I said, "Not in so many words. But from what I put together, she might have gone out on the beach during the blackout and started for Daskalos' place, then changed her mind."

"So she did lie when I asked about it. Why?"

"Because she still hasn't signed her movie contract," I said, and when Araujo looked puzzled I said, "I'll explain later. Right now you've got fifteen fast minutes of work ahead."

He made it in just under twenty minutes, and his

glum face told the story even before he dropped into his chair and gave me an almost imperceptible shake of the head.

One loaded gun still missing.

said, "Any chance of one of your blackouts tonight," he asked; which was not the kindest way to put it.

Coffee. Pastries. Fresh fruit and cheese. Liqueurs and that second-rate house brandy. A humidor of cigars was passed around. Toilet privileges, as Araujo had put it, were offered by our host. Most, including myself, took advantage of the offer.

Quist and Araujo kept me company in the lobby as the customers filed into the screening room, led by Calderon with Sharon in tow. When the corridor was cleared Quist said to me, "You'll probably have a dull time of it, but don't let that put you off-guard. About one thing especially. When it gets near twelve be watchful about anything Daskalos drinks. About anything that goes down his throat, for that matter."

"Poison?" I said. "What gives you that idea?"

"You may not take him at face value, but I do. And while I still can't guess what the hell he's up to, I believe he'll go to any lengths to achieve it."

"All right, I'll take that into account."

"But with restraint," Quist warned. "Nothing physical." He aimed a bony forefinger at me. "You know Mrs. Quist's regard for him. More than regard. I don't want anything done I'll have to apologize to her for."

"I'll take that into account too."

"That would be wise. Well, then. Keep close to him as long as you feel necessary, and that will be it. The plane'll be ready for you at ten in the morning. And you know your obligation to be discreet about events here. A practical joke which you easily cleared up. That's the story we're all agreed on."

"I've heard stranger ones."

"I'm sure." Quist abruptly shifted his attention to Araujo. "Any chance of one of your blackouts tonight?" he asked, which was not the kindest way to put it.

"No," said Araujo stiffly. "Not tonight. Absolutely not."

"I hope not." Quist started the wheelchair rolling. "All right, come along."

Araujo said, "In a moment, please." Looking as if he were ready to spit, he watched the chair swivel through the screening-room door with a thump. Then he said to me, "There's a cart outside for you. The man who brought it will be on duty here during the picture. Just let him know he's to take his post right now."

"Sure. By the way, are there any other doors in that movie house?"

"One. Behind the screen. Locked from the outside. Brand-new lock. And I'm the only one with the keys."

"Hang on to them," I said. "And keep counting those heads."

I gave the man outside his message, then traveled oceanward under the gas lamps at an easy pace. The wind wasn't what it had been—less gusty, much warmer and more humid, and now and then carrying the scent of flowers perking up and giving notice that the cold spell was on its way out.

I knocked on Daskalos' door, didn't expect any response, and didn't get any. I opened the door and walked in.

There were no lights on in the living room, but there was adequate lighting from another source. The fireplace was wide and deep. The fire in it had been built as high as possible. I could feel the heat of it across the room. And from across the room I could see the body stretched out on the floor just this side of the fire screen.

I moved toward it and switched on a standing lamp. Daskalos.

The late Daskalos.

On the run, crouching low, I knocked over the stand-ing lamp with the poker, and the bulb shattered, leav

He lay on his back staring at the ceiling with one eye. The other eye, where the bullet had taken him, was a bloody, blackened absence of eye. There was an added distortion of the face, too: One side of it gave the impression that, totally dead, he was howling his rage against what had happened. I looked closer. A denture, teeth gleaming, had been dislodged and protruded at an angle halfway out of his mouth.

I went into action fast—too fast—and almost flew arse over tip skidding on waxed floor as I headed for the kitchen phone. Wasted energy. The line was ripped out of the box. The line of the bedroom phone was ripped out of its base.

I went back to the living room and stood looking down at Daskalos, my mind spinning with the maddening futility of bald tires mired deep in gumbo. It was a log stacked too high on the fire which got my thinking untracked. The log shifted, teetered, and came rolling down that oversized pyre, landing almost up against the fire screen. Another inch and it would have toppled the screen across the body. I used the poker, scorching my hand in the process—the iron shaft was that hot—to give the smoldering wood clearance.

The log, my scorched hand, that eyeless eye suddenly all fitted together. And with that, everything else—all the pieces of the puzzle—fitted themselves together. Reject what couldn't be; accept what had to be. And when I did that I knew that I was in trouble.

I heard the sound at the front door and knew that the trouble had arrived, armed and ready.

On the run, crouching low, I knocked over the standing lamp with the poker, and the bulb shattered, leaving me in firelight. The question of what exactly had been going on at the door had two possible answers. I tried the knob and got the one that confirmed all suspicions. The door was now locked. A solid workmanlike door, too.

The windows? Keeping below sill level, I made an appraisal of one, then another. The layered look. A Venetian blind, those glass slats, mosquito screening, and last but definitely not least, an ornamental iron grille. Good for keeping people out. Unfortunately, just as good for keeping people in.

You think strange thoughts under pressure. Crouching there, poker in hand, I found myself thinking of that day I had lured Sharon, no dog lover, across the Devon line to Somerset to watch sheepdog trials. Nondescript animals to look at, responding to a few hand signals, they demonstrated an uncanny ability to round up scattered and panicky sheep and herd them into the designated den. For the first time now, I understood that the game might have been fun for the dogs, but it was sure as hell no fun for the sheep.

A crunching of gravel at the side of the building announced the next move in the game. I answered it at once, made it to the kitchen door ahead of grim destiny now crunching its way along the back wall. The kitchen door was unlocked. No bolt, no chain, a keyhole but no key. No surprise. Everything had been thought of. J. Milano, that beat-up, baffled ram was being invited to try escaping from his pen while right outside its gate the cleaver waited.

Beautiful. Strategy, tactics, and execution. Literally execution. All beautiful.

I looked around. There was enough moonlight filtering through the blinds to outline the two bottles Daskalos had kept handy for salad dressing, but not enough to clue me in on which was which. The first I uncapped reeked of vinegar. I opened the other, and starting from just inside the door, I backed away holding the bottle

167

upside down at arm's length, puddling the floor with oil. There wasn't much of it. It wouldn't have helped if there had been. My company was now at the door.

I slipped around the other side of the divider separating kitchen from dining room. I flattened my back against the divider, got a good grip on the poker, and tried to offer as little profile as possible as I watched the door start to open.

"Don't be foolish, Araujo," I called. "I have a gun, too."

N o you don't, Mr. Milano." He was all confidence. The door slowly opened wide. "There's never been one in your apartment; you don't carry one." Confident but not reckless. He wasn't strolling through that door until he could place me. "Mr. Milano?"

At all costs, he must not stroll in. He had to charge in.

I said, "My apartment? Would that be Pablo's report, by any chance?"

"Of course. A good boy. Very reliable." A shadowy hand appeared inside the door, and the ceiling light was switched on. It provided me with a clear and chilling view of the gun held in the other hand.

No time left. All I could depend on now was the natural impulse of the pursuer to follow the pace set by the pursued. I took a deep breath, banged the poker against the dividing wall to call for attention, then raced toward the living room with the feeling that here was a target painted on my back. I stopped and wheeled just in time to see Araujo go wildly off-balance on the oil slick. Leg's skewed, gun waving, he could have been the clown act at the ice show. But he didn't go down. I moved in, I put everything I could into that low, half-volley sweep of the poker into his leg, and down he went with a high-pitched scream. The gun skated like a hockey puck across the floor, and he lay stretched out on his back, spine arching. His face was agonized, his teeth sank so hard into his lower lip that an ooze of blood showed on it.

But there was another gun—there had to be—besides the one that had occupied the now-empty shoulder holster. I squatted down and opened his jacket, and there it was, tucked into his belt. I reached for it and didn't get to it. His arm suddenly locked around my neck like a vise, my head was crushed against his chest, my ear painfully grinding against a button there. I smelled not only sweat but graveyard dirt being readied for my coffin.

Snared in my own trap, I couldn't get leverage with my shoes on that oily surface. And I couldn't do more with my hands than hang on to his wrist when, with his free arm, he tried to reach the gun in his belt. So I did the only thing left to do. I managed to pivot my bursting head the necessary distance and sink my teeth into his jowl. I got a good solid mouthful of blubber in my jaws and clamped down on it like a maddened bulldog.

He didn't as much release me as fling me away, and I grabbed the gun as I went. I scrambled to my feet and leveled it at him. No need. He moved one leg feebly; the other was done for. And hurting. The swarthy face was slate-colored. The eyes were glazed with pain.

I used cord from the Venetian blind to lash his wrists together, arms over head, and anchor them to the base of the stove. The little effort required for this took the last of my strength. I made it to a chair and sat down. When I tried to light a cigarette I found that my hands were shaking so hard that I had to chase the lighter flame back and forth with the cigarette like a drunk before I got results.

Araujo said with an effort, "My leg."

"Hurts bad?" I asked, all sympathy.

"Yes."

"Well, if I had some of that painkiller you used on Quist's dog before you slit its throat, I'd be glad to give you a dose. But I don't have any. Too bad."

I took my time finishing the cigarette before I examined the leg. A clean break below the knee. I said, "You'll live. Of course, if you try anything, and that bone goes through the flesh and starts a hemorrhage, you might not."

The dull eyes brightened a little. Mind over matter. "Why would I try anything?" He licked the bloodied lower lip. "It's your story against mine. The best you can do is get away from here. I can help you. Money— whatever you need."

"Which leaves you to tell the whole sad story to the police, doesn't it? I took that gun from your man during the blackout—"

"You also made the blackout."

"Of course. And I hated Daskalos enough to kill him. You already have that idea circulating among our friends. So I finished off Daskalos with that stolen gun. And you showed up just in time to witness the murder and kill me when I tried to shoot you down in my getaway. Brave security chief does his duty when private eye goes berserk. Maybe even a medal from the mayor, right?"

"I have a man next door who'll swear—"

I cut in: "You don't have anybody next door. Not tonight. Why would you want someone around to testify that for twenty minutes during dinner, when you were supposed to be looking through a couple of apartments in the main building, you were right here in Daskalos' cottage? That time element was on your mind, and you covered it every way possible. In fact, you covered it too well."

"Too well?"

"That bonfire in there. I was supposed to have killed Daskalos ten minutes ago. But he was already two hours dead—and what if some shrewd medical examiner started wondering about that discrepancy? He's lying there cold and dead, and I'm lying there warm and dead. What to do? You overheat the room to make sure his body is kept nice and warm until the police take over. And that was the giveaway. That bonfire."

Araujo moved his head slowly from side to side. "None of this means anything. You're still in trouble."

"The story of my life."

"It'll be life in prison. Get away while you can. I'll help you."

I said, "I'll think about it. Meanwhile—"

He offered no resistance when I gagged him. Then I worked a length of cord through the trigger guards of both guns, hung them on a hook in the bedroom closet, locked its door, and pocketed its key. In the process I realized that my jacket and pants were stained with salad oil, my best jacket at that. But there's always a silver lining. After all, it could have been blood.

And all mine.

In the lobby, the security man—security boy, to go by his age—was sitting on the table keeping the punch-bowl mailbox company. He hastily stood up and gave me a stern, wide-awake look. I said, "All quiet?"

"Uh-huh." He nodded in the direction of the screening room. "Anyhow, nobody came out so far. Not after Mr. Araujo."

"Good. You know Miss Riley?"

"Oh, sure."

"Then, here's what Mr. Araujo wants you to do. You go in there very quietly and tell Miss Riley—but so nobody else can hear it—that he wants to see her in her office right away. Got that straight?"

"Uh-huh."

"Just say it into her ear and walk out. That's Mr. Araujo's orders. And if you're wondering why he's cutting it so fine, it's because anything you do or say differently is going to start trouble in there. Afterward, he's going to ask you why there was trouble."

"Ah, hey. He knows he can count on me."

"Just make sure he can."

I watched him approach the screening room. Then I moved quickstep down the hallway to the office and unlocked it with my all-purpose. Two minutes later, Maggie arrived breathless. She must have made the trip at a run. She stood in the doorway bewildered. "The man said it was Virgilio."

"I told him to. I figured otherwise you'd start wondering."

"I am wondering. Aren't you still supposed to be

with Kalos?" She frowned at me. "And what happened to your clothes?"

"Araujo's at the cottage, and never mind my clothes. Look, just come in and shut the door. Lock it."

Her eyes opened very wide. She said with foreboding, "Something's gone wrong."

"Yes." I drew her into the room and attended to the door myself.

"Kalos?"

"Dead. Araujo shot him. I've got Araujo roped up there."

She looked ready to pass out. I caught her around the shoulders and steered her to the chair facing the desk. She sagged into it and lowered her head almost to her knees. When she raised it the color was returning to her face. "Milano, don't just stand there looking at me like that. What happened? How did it happen?"

"You need a drink. So do I. If you tell me where Quist keeps that private stock—"

"No. I just want to hear what happened. Please."

I went around the desk and sat down in her chair. Her manuscript in its box was in the middle of the desk. I carefully put it to one side. Then, keeping it low-keyed, I described in detail everything that had happened after I walked into the cottage.

She was, as she had said, tough. Maggie Riley, girl of the Everglades. Tough-minded as well as tough-spirited. Her immediate response made that plain. "But aren't you in trouble? The way Virgilio said?"

"How?"

"It's your story against his. And you did have reason to hate Kalos. He didn't."

"I suppose not."

"Milano, don't you understand what I'm getting at? You're always talking about motive. Virgilio had no motive for the killing. It doesn't make sense that he did it."

"Wrong. He had half a million dollars' worth of motive. That's what he wanted Quist to invest in his Free Cuba movement. My guess is that Quist agreed to pay it in return for murder."

"Andrew? Are you saying *he* had something to do with it?"

"Everything. It's been his game from start to finish. And Daskalos was only a pawn sacrifice in it. Just like that pet dog that was butchered. And that security guy who got his skull cracked open. Because I'm the one Quist was out to get all along. John Milano, none other."

"That's paranoid!"

I said, "Baby, if I'm paranoid I've powerful good reason for it. How about those drinks now?"

Maggie came to her feet. "Never mind drinks. I want Andrew to hear all this."

"Not yet."

"If you're going to level charges at him—"

"I am. Now, sit down and I'll tell you why."

Unwillingly, she seated herself on the edge of the chair. "Well?"

I said, "As far as Quist is concerned, Sharon is the ultimate trophy. He is crackbrained, drooling possessive of her. Do you want to argue that point?"

"The language maybe. I'll concede the point."

"All right, then. Last July he found out the contents of that letter I returned to her. Later on, it was her Christmas letter. There it was. Clear evidence that she was determined to trade him in for me sooner or later. A powerful inducement for him to decide that the one permanent solution to the problem was to have me knocked off. When this movie crowd showed up—with Daskalos tagging along—he came up with a game plan."

Maggie said, "And having Kalos murdered was part of it? Kalos of all people? You are out of your mind. Andrew liked the way he kept Sharon in line. He told me so himself."

"He told me the same thing, and one of my mistakes was believing him. Because Sharon was already on her way to cutting loose from Daskalos, and Quist knew that. He had no more need or use for Daskalos at all.

"But this was only one of my mistakes. Another lay in not recognizing that Kalos, poor bastard, had come to believe his own preaching. Had really made the conversion. And was honestly trying to be protective of Sharon. I think Quist was shrewd enough to count on my not accepting that. One thing is sure. He never let me or anyone else here forget that I was violently antagonistic to Daskalos. A very important thing to have on the record when the bodies would be carted away."

"Of course," Maggie said in a flat voice. "All part of Andrew's satanic plan to have you knocked off."

"Whatever you want to call it, baby, it was one lovely plan from start to finish. He needed some kind of case as bait for me, so there were those threatening notes. To give substance to the threats, he had his dog killed. That would also keep me from suspecting him of any conniving, because what dog lover woud dream of having his faithful hound's throat cut? Then he pulled one of his cleverest moves. He set it up so that I'd think Sharon was inviting me down here. But as I learned from her this afternoon, she had been conned into mentioning my name and setting up the invitation. When I did arrive on the scene, all Quist had to do was keep me looking at everyone but him until I was set up for the kill. The son of a bitch came about thirty seconds from pulling it off, too."

Maggie sat there open-mouthed. Finally she said, "That's it?"

"That is it."

"Milano, do you realize how much of this is conjecture? How many holes there are in it?"

"Yes. Like conjecturing Quist somehow knew I hated Daskalos from long ago. Which would mean, after the smoke cleared away, that my murdering him was plausible. And since Araujo was then supposed to kill me in my attempted getaway, I couldn't disprove that. But if I get the answer to one simple question, I think all such holes would be plugged. Want to try answering it?"

"Why me? How about asking Andrew to try? Or are you afraid to confront him with this lunacy?"

"It really is a simple question. How did he know what was in Sharon's letters?"

"What makes you so sure he did?"

I said pleasantly, "Because you gave him that information. Just the way you told him everything Sharon confided to you. Your Andrew may be suffering from arrested moral development, baby, but he's nobody's fool. He knew exactly what he was marrying. But with you on the job, he'd never have to wonder what she was up to. He'd know about it as soon as she spilled it to you."

"My God," Maggie said. She regarded me with wonderment. "Do you hear yourself, Milano? The perfect frame-up. Concocted by Andrew Quist, who is not merely neurotically jealous but murderously jealous. Carried out by Virgilio Araujo for the sake of—how much did you say it was?"

"Half a million."

"Right. Half a million dollars which he needs to raise for the invasion of Cuba by his private army."

"You raise the army first," I pointed out. "The invasion comes later."

"Whenever. Both abetted by me, who provided necessary intelligence. For what reason I provided it, deponent sayeth not. Probably I was demonstrating a fierce loyalty to the murderous Quist."

I said, "Scratch the murderous Quist. Try Vincent van Gogh."

"What?"

"Van Gogh. You remember. That artist you're planning to do so much expensive research on."

"What about it?"

I said, "Well, fifty thousand dollars does buy a lot of research." I held up a hand. "Not that you're short-changing Quist. I mean, look what you're being paid for. Keeping tabs on Sharon. Attending to me personally to make sure your boss is always a step ahead of me. That drama when Kightlinger used your typewriter. And then the big one. The one you were scheduled for at the inquest. Telling the law with a straight face that after the bridge game last night you had no idea where I went to, but I certainly hadn't been with you. After all, if I had been, how could I have set off that blackout and swiped that gun to kill Daskalos with? You know, that lie alone would be worth the whole fifty thousand to Quist."

"Are you talking about my grant money?"

"Sure. What other jackpot is coming your way?"

"Then let me make very clear that this jackpot—if it does come my way—is not coming from Andrew. He had nothing to do with it in any shape, form, or fashion. Nothing at all."

"Not even a little something?"

"Nothing at all. That money is coming from a highly reputable Boston foundation that has my application and précis right there in its files. And whose return correspondence I have right here in my files."

"The Lucas Foundation," I said. When she blinked at that I said, "Sharon mentioned it."

"It was supposed to be confidential until the final decision. But that doesn't matter. What does matter is that you knew this would be a legitimate grant. So all your wild deductions—"

I said slowly, "Mary Henrietta Lucas Quist. The subject of that Sargent portrait in your museum. Quist's mother, so you told me. I haven't checked it out yet, but my wild deduction is that the Lucas Foundation is all Quist's. And, as it must have struck him, a very handy device for washing dirty money. Like money he'd have to pay someone for joining his conspiracy to commit murder."

Maggie stared at me. Her face was suddenly very white, the freckles blotchy on it. Then she said surprisingly, "Did you really think for one minute that I'd deny you were with me when that blackout started?"

I nodded sadly.

She stood up, and taking a pen from its holder and using a sheet of her manuscript paper, she leaned over the desk and wrote busily. I followed the words upside down.

To whom it may concern: John Milano was in my company at the time the blackout of Hesperides Estates occurred on January 23rd.

The signature was in the same minute, unadorned script: *Margaret Riley.*

She twisted the paper around on the desk so that it was right-side up from my angle, then sat down in a version of Sharon's schoolmarm position, shoulders squared, hands tightly clasped in her lap. One difference. The balls of her thumbs were pressed together. It gave her a prayerful look.

I rested my hand on the paper. "What is this? A small repayment for having set me up?"

"I expected that. No, it's proof of good faith, Milano. Beyond that, it's the preamble to a small confession. Yes, I did keep Andrew informed about Sharon. I wasn't happy about it from the start, but he insisted it was for her good, and somehow that made sense. But I never went beyond that. So help me God, I didn't know what he and Virgilio were up to. I didn't spy on you for him. I didn't write those notes to Kalos. You have to believe that, Milano. Is it so hard to believe?"

I said, "That new book about Bligh and the *Bounty* you had on the shelf there—you got rid of it, didn't you? Not that it matters. The price sticker had the store name on it. The Book Nook, Coconut Grove. Sounds like a cozy little place. I'm sure they'd remember selling it to you. Probably charged it to your account, for that matter."

"Milano—"

I said tiredly, "I was standing there looking down at Daskalos when I remembered where I saw that line before, the one in the first note to him. *I am in Hell*, capital *H* and all. It was what Fletcher Christian said to Bligh when he declared the mutiny. It would be in any authoritative book about the *Bounty*, so it had to be in that book you were reading, the one you borrowed it from. What's the sense of denying you wrote those notes when we both know you did? And you did report on me to Quist. And were part of his conspiracy."

She remained silent and unmoving, her brows knit, the edges of her teeth, just barely meeting each other, showing behind the retracted lips. She cocked her head at me. "What do you intend to do about it? You know that the kind of money Andrew would be willing to—"

"No."

"Totally incorruptible?"

"I doubt it. Just enough not to be bought off by somebody who tried to murder me."

"I see. Well, then?"

"It's up to you. When you're questioned, tell the truth. Offer to be a witness for the prosecution. A smart lawyer can plea bargain a good deal out of that." I came around the desk and handed her the phone. "It starts with a call to the police. It'll earn you points if you're the one to break the news to them. Whoever answers, tell him you want to report a murder, and make sure he's got your name right. Tell him to have the gateman here bring the responding officers straight to the screening room in the main building, where you'll be waiting. Oh yes, and tell him someone's badly hurt too, and needs an ambulance. That's it."

Not quite.

Eyes narrowed, Maggie was doing some heavy calculation. I rested my butt on a corner of the desk and waited. Finally she said, "I didn't have to write that." She motioned with her chin toward the sheet of paper on the desk. "Suppose I hadn't?"

"It wouldn't change anything."

"But it's your alibi, isn't it? What if I told the police you made me write it?"

I said, "I'll save you the trouble." I held up the paper, put my lighter to it, and after the flame had risen high I dropped it into the ashtray on the desk. Maggie, phone in hand, watched it smolder into ash. Her whole body seemed to go slack. She looked at me in confusion. "I thought—"

I said, "I have the murder weapon—that stolen gun with Araujo's fingerprints still on it—locked away. And Pablo, his nephew or whatever, planted your last note in the cottage, and he is not going to deny it long, once the cops start turning the screws. That's just for openers."

Kightlinger had said she packed a mighty wallop with her fist. She had better than a fist now, she had

180

that phone. The unexpected stunning impact of it high up against the side of my head sent me right off the desk to the floor. I didn't see stars. I saw massive astral bodies, constellations, galaxies, and beyond them, as I managed to get to hands and knees, I dizzily saw Maggie working the key in the terrace door. She got the door open, she was on her way through it, and she suddenly stopped and turned back.

It was her baby she had come for, the manuscript in its box on the desk. She was on her way again when I hit her with a shoulder tackle. Pages of manuscript flew one way, she flew another, and I went with her, desperately trying to grab whatever I could grab through that storm of fists and knees and hard-toed shoes. When I finally got her under control, flat on her belly, her arm twisted up behind her, she still strained to get free.

I put pressure on the arm, and she groaned. I could hear her breath rasping in her throat, each exhalation culminating in a barely audible whimper.

I said, "God damn it, get it into your head that I've been trying to do you a favor. I don't even know why. Maybe it's not you. Maybe it's Vincent van Gogh I want to do a favor for. But will you try to understand what I'm getting at?"

She made a noise in her throat.

I said, "All right, that didn't sound like no, so I'll take for granted it's yes. Now, listen close. When the showdown comes Quist will buy himself a dozen psychiatrists to swear him into a nice cushy sanitarium. Araujo's had it. He pulled the trigger, he goes up for life, maybe gets the chair. You are definitely not going to get the Quist treatment. And your one chance of not getting the Araujo treatment is in lining up with the prosecution."

She could barely manage to get it out. "And where does that leave me?"

"In very hot water," I said. "Which is still a lot better than boiling oil."

For a few moments I thought she had given up breathing altogether. "All right," she whispered at last, "I'll do it your way."

I helped her to her feet, with the feeling that I could have used the help at least as much as she did. I nudged her toward the phone. She balked at the sight of the papers all over the floor. "My book!"

"There's time for that later."

"No. Help me put it together. Then I'll make the call."

I helped her gather pages. She lovingly put them all together in order. Then she made the call.

T he young security man in the lobby looked puzzled. He said, "Mr. Araujo didn't come in." A question without a question mark.

I said, "It's all right. He just phoned he couldn't make it."

"Oh." He gave me a smile, started to give the somber Miss Riley a smile, then changed his mind. I smiled at him for both of us.

In the darkness of the screening room, I felt rather than saw us into the same seats against the back wall Sharon and I had occupied last evening. I slid down in my seat, resting on my aching spine, offering a minimum view in case anyone was curious about the door's brief opening.

No one, as far as I could make out from the silhouettes ahead, was. On the screen, Sharon was walking toward Nelson's Column in Trafalgar Square hand in hand with Calderon, who somehow looked smaller than he did in the flesh. So it was her last picture, the one she had made in London. And Quist, his wheelchair parked midway down the aisle, was watching his wife stop and hold up her face for an open-mouthed kiss from her screen lover while, I surmised, he must be gloating over the demise of her one-time real lover. A gaudy double turn-on for those sex instruction books.

Visibility increased as my eyes adjusted to the flickering light. Sharon sat beside Quist, head so far back against the seat that her profile was horizontal. Not sleeping, just rejecting the screen Sharon, who had everything going for her that the real Sharon didn't. Except for possibly those two weeks in a Devon cottage when they became one. Or had been close to becoming one.

Calderon sat a seat apart from Sharon, sending out smoke signals from an oversized cigar. Further down I could pick out the others. Belle Rountree's hand rested against the nape of her Scottie's neck. Lou Hoffman had his arm around his Alice in Wonderland's shoulders; she was plying a bottle of carbonated Drink Me. Kightlinger, alone in the first row, was hunched forward and seemed to be taking down notes on what he was watching. Or was it yet another appeal to his doctor friend for walking-around money? Same difference.

In a few minutes all hell was going to break loose here. First the police, then, not far behind, the press and TV. This happening was the kind they dreamed about. They'd be coming from Red China for it. They'd be all over it like roaches on a piece of stale cake.

On the screen, people in Trafalgar Square were eyeing the lovers. Calderon said to Sharon with heavy humor, "It doesn't take much to draw a crowd here, does it?"

Sharon looked at him gravely. The camera moved close to that face. She slowly shook her head. "I don't see any crowd."

I looked at the real Sharon. Horizontal or otherwise—especially horizontal—that profile long ago would have launched at least a thousand ships.

Milano, the profile freak. Appreciate it, but under no conditions let it get to you.

On the screen, very close up, the sapphire eyes glowed, the lips parted.

I closed my eyes. No use. I opened them again.

So all hell was going to break loose here any minute. When it was over and done with, accounts settled, witnesses dismissed—let Willie Watrous threaten a coronary, let Shirley Glass shake her head in despair—I would arrange for two weeks in Devon with that profile. And, God help me, everything else that went with it.

That would be our clear, hard understanding. Two weeks, and absolutely no more.

At the most, three.

About the Author

STANLEY ELLIN has been called "a master storyteller."
His novels have been translated into twenty languages
and have won him an international reputation. He
has been honored with seven Edgar Allan Poe awards;
and his works have been made into movies by such
directors as Joseph Losey, Clive Donner and Claude
Chabrol, and into numerous television plays, most
notably by Alfred Hitchcock. Mr. Ellin is married,
and his year is divided between his homes in New
York and Miami Beach.